Bone-Chiller!

A COMEDIC MYSTERY-THRILLER

by Monk Ferris

G000138453

SAMUEL FRENCH, INC.

45 WEST 25TH STREET   NEW YORK 10010

7623 SUNSET BOULEVARD   HOLLYWOOD 90046

LONDON   *TORONTO*

CAST OF CHARACTERS

JERRY DELVIN, a soon-to-be groom—with an odd job
CONNIE TRAVERS, his soon-to-be terrified fiancee
BUZZY BURDETT, their very baffled buddy
THEODOSIA TRAVERS, Connie's stepmother
FLAME FONDUE, a kindergarten teacher?!
ZITA VAN ZOK, a very unorthodox lady's-companion
MAUVINS, the Travers' family butler
*ADLER SHERIDAN, The Travers' family lawyer
KISSY TRAVERS, Connie's excitable teen-aged sister
ELOISE AINSLEY, Theodosia's highly agitated sister
PIPPI, the Travers' family maid
*LUCRETIA, the Travers' family cook
"DAN DENTON," a friend of Flame's—or is he?

*[NOTE: The foregoing 5 males and 8 females can be altered to 4 males and 9 females by making "ADLER" into "ADDIE"—or be altered to 6 males and 7 females by making "LUCRETIA" into "LUCENTIO".]

TIME: The Present
LOCALE: The parlor/library of the Travers family mansion in New York City

ACT ONE: About 7 P.M. on a Friday the 13th
ACT TWO: About midnight, the same day
ACT THREE: About ten minutes later

Bone-Chiller!

ACT ONE

Curtain rises on the parlor/library of the Travers mansion in New York City. While the "Stage Setting" page provides the general layout, here are certain particulars you should know: Lightswitches #1 and #3 control all *lights onstage, including front hall, so "LIGHTS GO OUT" means* total *darkness [Lightswitch #2 is never used]; the painting that masks the wall safe is of [left-to-right] the face of Sandra [or Ruby or Frances] Dee, a large paw with a large pimple, and, cheek-to-cheek, Barbara [or Catherine] Bach and Johann Sebastian Bach; the secret panel above the phonograph is a square 1' × 1', one of many surrounding identical wood-panel squares, and is about 5' above floor-level; besides the stuffed bird [on a 4'-high single-legged table], there should be at least 6 more items of taxidermy in the room [animal heads on walls, perhaps, or some smaller fauna on small tables, or both; suit yourself]; and, for reasons that will become clear in the final act, there is needed at least 10' of wing-space in back of that secret panel.*

At curtain-rise, stage is empty; room-lighting is bright and cheery. DOOR CHIMES SOUND. After a moment, PIPPI—a 30ish young lady in maid's uniform— enters D.R. *via kitchen door and stands immobile, keeping door ajar, looking toward archway.*

LUCRETIA. (*off* D.R.) Is someone getting the door, Pippi?

PIPPI. (*calls back into kitchen*) Not so far, Lu. Should *I* go?

LUCRETIA. (*off* D.R.) A parlormaid has no business answering doors.

(*MAUVINS, a past-middle-age stately butler — moving at his typical snail's pace — appears in archway from* R., *moving majestically toward front door.*)

PIPPI. Oh, it's okay, Lu. Mauvins is getting it. (*starts back into kitchen*)

LUCRETIA. (*off* D.R. *before door quite swings shut again*) That could take all night!

(*And indeed, before MAUVINS reaches front door, DOOR CHIMES SOUND again; he halts, annoyed, and then takes the final two steps needed to reach door and opens it; we hear WIND HOWLING outside front door as ELOISE AINSLEY, a middle-aged lady bundled up against the cold, hurries into the hall, starts doffing topcoat.*)

MAUVINS. (*closing door — which will CUT OFF WIND-HOWLING*) Good evening, Miss Ainsley. (*will assist her out of her topcoat, during:*)

ELOISE. It's anything *but* good, Mauvins! I suspect we're in for a blizzard! The wind-chill outdoors feels like ninety below!

MAUVINS. The evening *is* tending toward the inclement, yes.

(*Both will enter parlor, now, he to hang her coat in closet, she to go behind bar and pour herself a fairly stiff drink, their dialogue continuing uninterrupted as they do so:*)

ELOISE. Am I the first?

MAUVINS. Mister Sheridan has been here about twenty minutes or so, I believe. His hair was somewhat wind-blown and he went to the small bathroom at the rear of the hall to effect repairs. (*is out of closet by now, and shuts door*)

ELOISE. Hasn't Theodosia come downstairs yet?

MAUVINS. (*moving toward archway, pauses for:*) Your sister, I believe, is changing her gown, Miss Ainsley.

ELOISE. Probably for the fourteenth time, if I know Theo! I don't know who she thinks she's going to impress! (*has come down around front of bar, now, with drink in hand, and notices chart—at the moment, rolled up into a cylinder, like a windowshade—on wall*) What in the world is that? (*points*)

MAUVINS. (*looks where she is pointing*) I have no idea, Miss. Mister Sheridan fastened it up there when he first arrived, and instructed me to allow no one to touch it.

ELOISE. (*intrigued, moves toward it*) How strange! (*reaches for pull-tab in lower center of chart*) Let's have a look, shall we?

MAUVINS. But Miss Ainsley—

ELOISE. Now-now, no qualms, Mauvins! You did as instructed. I have been informed not to touch it. That I do not choose to *obey* that instruction is no reflection on you! (*reaches for pull-tab again*)

ADLER. (*comes around R. end of archway, steps into parlor*) Ah-ah-ah! Naughty-naughty! (*He is a man of about the same age as MAUVINS, but a lot more brisk and imposing of manner.*)

ELOISE. (*annoyed*) Adler! I only wanted a peek at whatever you're being so mysterious about.

ADLER. Even at the risk of your inheritance?

ELOISE. (*withdraws her hand from pull-tab instantly*) What? Are you saying this thing has some connection with Uncle Josiah's will?

ADLER. As a matter of fact, it *is* Josiah's will!

ELOISE. What, on a roll-up chart? Isn't that a bit— unusual?

ADLER. (*will move to bar and fix himself a drink, during:*) Josiah Travers was not a usual man.

MAUVINS. (*who has begun to feel like an eavesdropper*) If you will excuse me—? (*takes step toward archway*)

ELOISE. You may as well stay, Mauvins. After all, the reading of the will is scheduled for eight o'clock—if you go all the way back to the servants' quarters at *your* normal speed, you'll *never* make it back here in time. (*As he hesitates, DOOR CHIMES SOUND; he looks that way, takes a step, but stops as ELOISE hurries past him toward front door.*) Relax, Mauvins, *I'll* get the door! (*He will turn, uncertainly, then move slowly—as he almost* always *moves—to a point* D.L. *near phonograph.*)

ADLER. (*coming down around end of bar with drink*) I'd better go and get the rest of the staff . . . (*He will move* D.R. *to kitchen door during:*)

ELOISE. (*opening front door*) Come in, come in, before you freeze solid!

(*NOTE: HOWLING WIND will* always *be heard whenever front door is opened, and will cease whenever it shuts.*)

ADLER. (*has pushed kitchen door* R., *slightly, calls through gap:*) Lucretia—? Pippi? We're almost ready to start!

(*As he lets door swing to, and starts toward archway, FLAME FONDUE—a totally gorgeous young woman in her mid-20s—hurries in through front door, clutching her topcoat closed at the neck, shivering, as ELOISE closes door.*)

FLAME. I *hope* this is the Travers residence? 'Cause if it's not, I'm staying here anyhow! That weather's not fit for polar bears! (*has removed her topcoat during speech, now hands it to a surprised ELOISE, moves down into parlor*) Is there a glass of brandy on the premises? (*spots bar, heads there at once*) Hurray, an oasis! Mind if I help myself? (*doesn't wait for a reply, is already fixing drink*)

ELOISE. (*with stiff politeness, has come into parlor and almost opens closet door—then propriety takes the helm, and she moves instead down to MAUVINS, handing him the coat, and moves toward bar as he moves toward closet*) I don't believe we've been introduced. . . ?

FLAME. I don't believe it either. (*takes sip of brandy, then extends hand to ELOISE*) I'm Flame Fondue. Who are you?

ELOISE. (*allowing FLAME to pump her hand up and down in a vigorous handshake, but applying no assistance to it*) I'm—Eloise Ainsley, Mrs. Travers' sister . . . but I'm afraid I don't recognize your name at all, Miss—Fondue, was it?

FLAME. (*nods*) Still is! (*ceases handshaking, takes another sip of drink*) Is there an Adler Sheridan here?

ADLER. (*who has been standing near desk, enjoying the episode*) *I* am Adler Sheridan, Miss Fondue. So glad you could make it.

FLAME. (*shrugs*) Friday nights are easy—I don't have to get up for work in the morning.

ELOISE. What sort of work do you *do*, Miss Fondue?

FLAME. I'm a kindergarten teacher. And you can call me "Flame."

ELOISE. Adler, I don't understand. I mean—I had assumed tonight would be just—*family* . . .

ADLER. I am merely following your late uncle's instructions, Eloise. He left a list of names, and was most specific about who should come.

ELOISE. I see. Miss—I wonder—that is—? Could you explain how—um—

FLAME. How *I* knew Josie?

ELOISE. "Josie"? Do you mean Uncle Josiah?

FLAME. Well, I could hardly call him that, seeing as he wasn't my uncle, now could I?! Come to think of it— how come *you* do? I mean, he wasn't *your* uncle either.

ELOISE. (*stiffly*) I always *thought* of him as such! And he practically *was*—I mean—well—he was the uncle of my dear sister Theodosia's late husband Charles. So you see—

FLAME. I see that, family-wise, you're no more his relative than *I* am!

ELOISE. You have no right to say that!

FLAME. Just because it's a fact?

ADLER. Now-now, ladies, there's no need to squabble—(*glances* D.R. *as PIPPI, followed by LUCRETIA, a stout woman of about 40, enters from kitchen; he adds quickly, in a lowered voice:*)—especially in front of the servants!

LUCRETIA. Are we starting pretty soon? I've got a crown roast of lamb in the oven!

FLAME. Darn! And I grabbed me a Big Mac on the way over! (*to ADLER*) You should've *told* me there'd be refreshments!

(*DOOR CHIMES SOUND.*)

MAUVINS. (*who has closeted FLAME's coat by now*) Excuse me—(*starts toward archway*)

ADLER. *I'll* get it, Mauvins! Why don't you and the others sit down and get comfortable?

(*As he starts toward front door, MAUVINS will sit on footstool and PIPPI and LUCRETIA close together near L. end of sofa—this trio is not used to being seated in the presence of their superiors, of course, so each in his/her own way is a bit uneasy about it; FLAME will sit on barstool facing down into room, and ELOISE will approach her there; all this happens during:*)

MAUVINS. Doesn't seem fitting, somehow . . .

LUCRETIA. But I've been on my feet all day . . .

PIPPI. And it *is* rather special circumstances . . .

ELOISE. Miss Fondue, you never *did* tell me how you happened to know my uncle . . .

FLAME. It's nothing juicy. Really, honey.

ELOISE. I never said—

FLAME. But you were thinking.

(*ADLER has front door open, now, and JERRY DEL-VIN and BUZZY BURDETT hasten in, removing topcoats even as ADLER is re-closing door; both are in mid-20s, and pleasant of aspect.*)

JERRY. Hi, I'm Jerry Delvin.

BUZZY. Buzzy Burdett.

JERRY. Hope we're not late. It took forever to find a taxi.

ADLER. (*takes their coats*) We can't begin till everyone is present, anyhow. (*starts toward closet*) Come in and get comfortable while you're waiting.

JERRY. (*as he and BUZZY enter parlor*) Who else is coming?

ADLER. (*business of hanging up coats, etc.*) Just one more from outside. The others are still upstairs.

FLAME. Well, *hello* there! Can I offer you a drink?

ELOISE. (*annoyed by this stranger's offer of hospitality*) Really, Miss Fondue!

JERRY. "Fondue"?

FLAME. "Flame."

BUZZY. I'd love to!

ELOISE. It's her *name*!

BUZZY. (*during business of him and JERRY getting drinks, looks around room in interested curiosity*) What *is* this place, a *parlor* or a *pet* cemetery?

ELOISE. My late brother-in-law, Charles, did taxidermy as a hobby. Quite adept at it, really. Oh, but I'm forgetting my manners—I am Eloise Ainsley, and this is Pippi our parlormaid . . . Lucretia our cook . . . Mauvins our butler . . .

ADLER. (*just finished with coats, closing closet door*) And I am Adler Sheridan, the late Josiah Travers' lawyer.

JERRY. (*after he and BUZZY acknowlege intros with nods, waves, etc.*) So *you're* Aunt Eloise!

ELOISE. I *beg* your pardon!

BUZZY. Why, what'd you *do*?

JERRY. I'm sorry for the familiarity, Eloise. It's just that *Connie* always calls you that.

ELOISE. (*taken aback*) I wasn't aware you *knew* my niece!

BUZZY. I *hope* he does—they're getting *married* in two weeks!

ELOISE. That's *impossible*!

JERRY. Well—"improbable," perhaps, I'll grant you. Say, where *is* Connie?

ELOISE. Now, just a moment—! (*Unnoticed by her, a foursome descends the stairs and enters the parlor: THEODOSIA TRAVERS, a handsome woman of middle age; CONNIE TRAVERS, a lovely young woman in her mid-twenties; KISSY TRAVERS, Connie's attractive sister, about 18 or 19; and ZITA VAN ZOK, a small woman of indeterminate middle age, garbed rather flamboyantly in "gypsyish" style—bright skirt and blouse, shawl, lots of earrings, rings, bracelets, etc.; ELOISE, meantime, is continuing without pause:*) My niece Connie is in the Social Register!

JERRY. (*pleasantly*) And *I'm* merely in the Manhattan phone book, is *that* it?

ELOISE. I must admit—the name "Jerry Delvin" means absolutely *nothing* to me. . . !

BUZZY. (*shrugs*) It's not *his* fault you don't do crossword puzzles!

ELOISE. I beg your pardon?

BUZZY. *Now* what'd you do?

CONNIE. Aunt Eloise, that's how Jerry makes his living!

ELOISE. (*turns, sees newcomers*) Oh! I hadn't realized you'd all come down yet. But—?

THEO. Eloise, will you *relax*? Uncle Josiah introduced them, himself! You *know* how fond he was of puzzles!

ELOISE. Well, yes, but—

KISSY. Don't be such a party-poop, Auntie! A good puzzle constructor can make a *very* nice living at it. (*to BUZZY*) Hi! I'm Kissy!

BUZZY. You sure are!

CONNIE. Buzzy, that's short for "Kirsten"! Don't get any ideas!

BUZZY. Too late! (*to KISSY*) May I fix you a drink?

CONNIE. My sister's under twenty-one.

KISSY. That's never stopped me before!

BUZZY. (*already heading for bar*) I'll put in a lot of soda.

THEO. Doesn't that get the alcohol into the bloodstream even faster?

BUZZY. (*with a semi-insane grin*) You're reading my mind! (*business of fixing drink for KISSY, during:*)

ELOISE. (*almost in tears, moves to THEO*) Who *are* all these people?! I thought tonight was for family!

ZITA. (*laughs almost harshly; OTHERS look her way*) You fear losing your share of the Travers millions, don't you! The more people in the will, the less money to go around! (*ELOISE almost protests, but stops as ZITA holds up an imperious hand.*) But . . . I tell you—I tell *all* of you—this is *not* an ordinary will!

ADLER. (*who, since hanging up coats, has made his way to a spot between chair and desk, but has not sat down*) Zita, don't be ridiculous! You cannot *possibly* know the terms of—

ZITA. (*interrupts serenely*) I knew Josiah Travers. A man like that would *not* make an ordinary will!

CONNIE. I hate to say it, but she's probably right!

ZITA. Have I ever been wrong?

THEO. (*unhappily*) Not so long as *I've* known you . . . (*to the JERRY/BUZZY/FLAME group, still near bar*) And Zita has been my companion for most of my adult life!

KISSY. That *is* a long time!

ELOISE. Really, Kirsten!

FLAME. Hold it, things are going a little too fast for me—could I have a go-round of the names again?

BUZZY. Maybe they should've printed up programs.

ADLER. Here, let *me* do it, for *everyone's* benefit . . .

ELOISE. No, wait—just putting *names* to people isn't enough! *I* should like to know *why* certain persons are here!

JERRY. Isn't this gathering by invitation only?

ELOISE. Well, *yes*, but—

ADLER. I believe Eloise is trying to sort out in her mind what possible *reason* there might be for certain of those invitations.

JERRY. Oh, *now* I get it! Well, here, let *me* start: I'm Jerry Delvin. I make my living creating puzzles for a variety of magazines. I met Josiah Travers one day when he came to my office to complain about an erroneous definition I'd given for a puzzle-clue. He was very big on puzzles—

THEO. He certainly was. We could barely keep him supplied with enough magazines to satisfy him.

ELOISE. Even so, the world must be *full* of puzzle-creators—why should Uncle Josiah have singled out Mister Delvin to share in what should be a *family* inheritance?

JERRY. (*shrugs*) For that matter, why did he insist on having Mister Sheridan invite *Buzzy*? Buzzy never even *met* him!

FLAME. Then how did he even know Buzzy *existed*?

ZITA. Obviously, as a friend of Jerry's, his name cropped up in the investigator's report.

CONNIE. (*apprehensive*) *Zita!*

JERRY. (*to CONNIE, not very pleased*) Your great-uncle had me *investigated*?! Why didn't you tell me?

CONNIE. I was afraid you'd be upset.

JERRY. You were right! The nerve of him, snooping and prying into my—

THEO. Jerry, it's a common practice in wealthy families, to be certain that marriageable offspring don't fall prey to fortune-hunters.

JERRY. (*very disappointed, to CONNIE*) Well, *thanks* a *lot*!

CONNIE. Jerry, honey, *I* didn't sick those detectives on you!

BUZZY. Of course she didn't, Jer! Give her a break, huh!?

JERRY. (*sees the sense in this*) Aw—hell—I'm sorry, Connie. But you should've *told* me about it!

ELOISE. I'd *still* like to know how these two *became* engaged! Where did they meet? When did they—

CONNIE. The same day *Josiah* met Jerry, Aunt Eloise. He didn't *drive*, you must remember. I was playing chauffeur for him that day, and we all went out to lunch —Jerry, Josiah and myself—to argue about puzzle-clues and such, and—well—one thing led to another, and—

FLAME. *Wait* a minute, *wait* a minute! (*when OTHERS look her way:*) I *didn't* want anybody's entire *autobiography*! I just wanted to know who's who.

ELOISE. And *I* merely wished to know what connection anyone had with Josiah.

ADLER. Then let's keep it simple. We've covered Jerry and Buzzy fairly well—Josiah admired Jerry's line of work and—for reasons known only to Josiah himself— also insisted we invite Jerry's best friend Buzzy to this gathering tonight.

ELOISE. (*to BUZZY*) Then *you*'re *not* in the puzzle-business?

BUZZY. Not even close. I'm a pediatrician!

FLAME. A *children's* doctor? How interesting! *I* teach kindergarten!

BUZZY. (*warmly*) I *knew* we must have something in common! You teach the tots, I give 'em shots!

ADLER. (*irked by the constant side-tracking*) Mister Burdett, may I remind you we're gathered for the reading of a *will—not* to hold auditions for *The Dating Game*!

BUZZY. You sound disappointed.

KISSY. Actually, I think he's jealous.

CONNIE. Kissy!

(*DOOR CHIMES SOUND.*)

KISSY. Saved by the bell! (*hastens toward archway*) I'll get it!

ELOISE. (*almost in despair*) Whom *else* are we expecting?!

ADLER. (*soothingly*) Just one more, Eloise, then we can get down to business. (*KISSY is now opening front door.*) This should be Daniel Denton, the final guest on the list.

FLAME. (*startled*) *Dan Denton?* But—(*As others stare at her, she controls herself a bit.*) Sorry. Didn't mean to shout.

(*DAN DENTON, 30ish, not un-handsome, is by now inside entry, removing topcoat while KISSY closes front door.*)

BUZZY. Then why *did* you?

FLAME. It's—nothing, Buzzy. Nothing at all.

DAN. (*entering parlor*) Good evening. I'm Daniel Denton.

THEO. Here, let me take your coat, Mister Denton. (*as she does so and starts for closet:*) I'm Theodosia Travers.

KISSY. (*just entering parlor behind him*) And I'm

Kissy. (*extends hand*) *Very* happy to make your acquaintance, I'm sure.

ELOISE. Kirsten, when *I* was a young lady, it was considered *unseemly* for a girl to speak to a man without being properly introduced!

KISSY. What good did *that* do?

DAN. (*while a flabbergasted ELOISE tries to think of an answer*) Glad to meet you, Kissy. (*as he shakes her still-extended hand:*)

ADLER. Now that we're all here, perhaps we can begin —? (*starts to sit down at desk*)

ZITA. Not so fast! We *still* have a lot of identifying to do!

ADLER. (*wearily stands up again*) I thought you *mystical* types *knew* everything *without* being told!

ZITA. (*carelessly*) Nobody's perfect.

ADLER. Look, why don't you all find seats, and we can get matters under way, please?

(*Over next few speeches, group will arrange themselves as follows: ZITA will sit in armchair u. of where MAUVINS still sits on footstool; THEO and ELOISE will sit on sofa beside PIPPI and LUCRETIA; FLAME, BUZZY, KISSY, CONNIE and JERRY will perch on barstools, but facing toward ADLER at desk, and DAN will stand uncertainly in area between archway and sofa.*)

ZITA. *I'm* taking the *comfortable* chair!

THEO. (*moving from closet where she has just hung up DAN's coat*) Eloise, why don't you join me on the sofa?

ELOISE. Next to the *servants*?!

THEO. I'll act as a buffer, dear. (*will sit between ELOISE and servants*)

DAN. (*as OTHERS perch on barstools*) I guess the cheese stands alone!

BUZZY. (*to ADLER*) You sure we're not here for Musical Chairs?

ADLER. (*ignoring BUZZY with an effort, says to DAN:*) There's the coffeetable — if you don't mind —?

DAN. (*moving that way*) I don't mind if you don't. (*will sit on R. end of coffeetable facing desk, during:*)

ELOISE. Those legs aren't very sturdy. Why don't you swap with one of the servants?

LUCRETIA. We were here first!

THEO. Really, Lucretia!

DAN. I don't mind. Honestly I don't.

(*Then a LOUD BUZZING comes from kitchen,* D.R.)

LUCRETIA. (*bounds to her feet*) My roast! (*starts* D.R. *almost at a run*) Excuse me!

BUZZY. Now's your *chance*, Dan!

THEO. You may as well, Mister Denton. *Anything* to get matters over with!

(*DAN, a little embarrassed, shrugs and moves to the spot vacated by LUCRETIA, who has exited* D.R.)

ZITA. Adler, can we *please* get on with it? We can always fill Lucretia in *later*!

PIPPI. That's not *fair*, just because she has to *cook* for the lot of you! (*to ZITA*) Why don't *you* go take care of dinner, and we'll fill *you* in later?!

ELOISE. Pippi, you are forgetting your place!

THEO. Nonsense, Eloise, even *servants* have feelings! (*to PIPPI*) But you *are* speaking out of turn, dear.

PIPPI. (*somewhat mollified*) Sorry, ma'am.

ADLER. (*a bit sardonically*) Now that domestic harmony reigns supreme again, may we—

CONNIE. Adler, there's no call to be snotty!

KISSY. Look, while we're waiting for Lucretia, why don't we finish that exposé we started a moment ago?

ELOISE. Thank you, Kirsten. That's very thoughtful of you.

KISSY. Not really. I guess I'm just as nosy as *you* are!

ADLER. (*near the snarling point*) All *right*! Let's *have* the roll-call—but be *brief* about it! Now, Jerry and Buzzy have been explained—

DAN. Not to *me* . . .

ADLER. (*controls an urge to shout, takes a breath, then sags wearily down into desk chair*) Very well. (*with an almost-dismissive wave of the hand toward bar*) Take it from the top!

JERRY. Okay. I'm Jerry Delvin, a puzzle-constructor. Josiah loved to do puzzles. I presume *that's* why he invited me.

BUZZY. I'm Buzzy Burdett, a pediatrician. Since there are no tiny tots on the premises, I have to assume I'm here because Jerry's my best friend. Doesn't make sense, but there it is.

FLAME. I'm Flame Fondue, and I teach kindergarten. I met Josie—that is, Mister Travers—at an assembly meeting at my school, when he was guest of honor—he donated a new wing to the school, and that's why he was there—to make the formal motions of turning over the check. I must have made an impression on him, I guess.

BUZZY. So we know he was of sound mind!

ELOISE. Mister Burdett—!

BUZZY. Sorry. It slipped out.

CONNIE. Well, *I'm* here because—well—I'm Connie Travers, Josiah's grandniece and—well—I *live* here!

KISSY. Same goes for me—except I'm Kissy, not Connie, of course.

THEO. Your turn, Eloise.

ELOISE. But why should *I* have to—

BUZZY. You made *us* do it!

ELOISE. Ohhh . . . very well. I am Eloise Ainsley, sister of Theodosia Travers, who was the wife of the late Charles Travers, the nephew of Josiah. I am here by invitation—because I'm a family member, I suppose.

THEO. And I'm the Theodosia she just mentioned. I married Charles about ten years ago, when he was a widower with two young daughters to raise. Charles died about five years ago, and—well, I've raised Connie and Kissy and—well—I *live* here!

PIPPI. I'm Pippi Dixon, the parlormaid. I work here.

MAUVINS. And I am Mauvins, the butler. I work here, too.

ZITA. I am Zita Van Zok. I have been Theo's friend and companion for many years. I came here to live when Charles passed away.

ADLER. And Lucretia, who just went running out of here, is the family cook, of course. Does that cover everybody?

JERRY. All except Dan Denton. (*Others look expectantly toward DAN.*)

DAN. This—this is rather embarrassing—

BUZZY. Should the ladies leave the room?

DAN. No-no, it's nothing like that. It's just—well—my name is Dan Denton—I never met Mister Josiah Travers in my life—and I haven't even the *faintest* idea why *I* was invited here tonight!

ADLER. Really? How very odd! I would have thought—that is—well, as Josiah's longtime lawyer, I still could not be expected to know *all* of his acquaintances, but—he specifically requested that *you* be in *attendance*, Mister Denton.

ELOISE. Wait—! Perhaps it's not who Mister Denton *is*, but what he *does*. (*when OTHERS look toward her in puzzlement*) I mean, Josiah would send for, say, a *plumber*, without knowing the man *personally*, if you follow me—? So perhaps—?

JERRY. Hey, that makes good sense. And, come to think of it, you never *did* tell us *what* you are, Denton . . .

DAN. Only because I couldn't imagine what possible *bearing* it would have on my presence here.

BUZZY. Just what *do* you do, then?

FLAME. *I* can tell you that! Dan Denton is a plain-clothes policeman, working out of the *homicide* division!

ELOISE. Oh, no! (*surprisingly, bursts into tears*) I thought we were all *over* that!

THEO. (*comforting her*) There-there, Eloise, I'm *sure* it's merely some sort of coincidence!

JERRY. *What* is?

BUZZY. All over *what*?

DAN. Then—you don't *know*—?

CONNIE. I never *told* Jerry. It was so—so awful—and the newspapers were not given the details, and the police commissioner was kind enough to keep the thing under wraps, as a favor to the family—

THEO. He and Josiah had been very close friends—

JERRY. Whoa! *What* details?

BUZZY. Keep *what* under wraps?

FLAME. Yeah, what's going *on* around here, anyhow?

KISSY. You may as well know the truth —

ELOISE. Kirsten — !

THEO. No-no, she's right. It *has* to come out some-time.

BUZZY. *Not* at the rate it's *going!*

JERRY. Connie — what have you been keeping from me?

CONNIE. Uncle Josiah — the *way* he died. You assumed it was old age, and — well — I let you go *on* assuming it.

JERRY. *Assuming?!* Connie, you *told* me your great-uncle had died quite peacefully in his bed!

CONNIE. Well — he *did* — in a way . . .

BUZZY. *What* way?

KISSY. Somebody chopped him up with a meat-cleaver! Into seventeen pieces!

(*Then all look abruptly* D.R. *as LUCRETIA re-enters, wiping her hands on her apron; she senses their combined focus, stops, looks uncertain and uneasy.*)

BUZZY. (*after a moment's silence*) I can see what Connie meant by *piecefully* — except I was *spelling* it wrong!

JERRY. Do you mean — *murder?!*

BUZZY. Jerry, a meat-cleaver is hardly *natural* causes! And *nobody* would commit *suicide* that way!

LUCRETIA. (*finally catches the gist of their conversation*) Oh! You're all doing it *again!* *Why* must you keep dragging it up, *why*!? I tell you, I had *nothing* to *do* with it! *Nothing!* (*bursts into tears, exits* D.R. *to kitchen*)

PIPPI. (*jumps up and rushes after her*) *Now* see what you've all done! Lu! Lu, you don't understand — ! (*exits*)

FLAME. What did Lucretia *mean*?

ADLER. It was *her* meat-cleaver that did the job. Fortunately, it was her night off, and she had a solid alibi . . .

THEO. Besides, *anyone* could have gotten that cleaver from the kitchen. We don't keep them locked *up*, or anything . . .

DAN. Do you mean it's still hanging there, where anybody might just—

CONNIE. Oh, no! We threw it away after—uh—afterward.

ELOISE. Didn't seem right, somehow, using it to fix meals after it had been used for—well—

MAUVINS. So these days we purchase our meat ready-cut.

DAN. I don't *blame* you!

(*Then all look around in puzzlement as a steady BEEP-BEEP is heard, finally focusing on BUZZY, who all at once jumps down from barstool and removes a beeper from his pocket and quickly turns it off.*)

BUZZY. (*moving deskward*) A pediatrician's day is never done! May I use your phone?

ADLER. Really, Mister Burdett, if we are *ever* to get the will read—!

CONNIE. Adler, you can't start without Lucretia and Pippi anyhow!

ADLER. (*rises from chair as BUZZY starts to dial*) You're right, of course, Connie. Let me try to get them back . . . (*will exit to kitchen during:*)

JERRY. Listen, while we're waiting, I'm kind of curious how it is that a kindergarten teacher is acquainted with a detective out of homicide.

FLAME. That's easy. We belong to the same aerobics class.

KISSY. How disappointing. *I* was hoping you'd met on a *professional* basis!

FLAME. Sorry. I haven't murdered anybody in weeks and weeks—

DAN. —and I'm too tall for kindergarten.

BUZZY. (*has his party by now, and OTHERS listen in interest as he speaks on phone:*) Hello, Doctor Burdett here . . . Oh, I see . . . Yes, put me through . . . (*pauses a moment; then:*) This is Doctor Burdett. What seems to be the problem? . . . Oh, damn! How did it happen? . . . Uh-huh . . . Yes, I guess some adhesive tape on the neck—at least for now . . . Oh, really? . . . Which foot? . . . And the left ear, too?! . . . How *many* pieces? . . . Heck, *I* don't know . . . You'd better get a *specialist* . . . Well, if you really think you *can* . . . Yeah, sure, why not! . . . Sure, but if Elmer's Glue won't do it, I don't think there's much hope . . . Yeah, keep me posted . . . Right. 'Bye. (*hangs up, notices OTHERS staring at him in mute fascination; explains:*) My nurse dropped an antique vase.

(*As they react, ADLER re-enters from kitchen, with a solicitous PIPPI guiding a still-sniffling LUCRE-TIA; DAN will get up from sofa and allow the two women to take their former places there, and AD-LER will return to desk chair and sit, during:*)

JERRY. I'd *still* like to know how Josiah happened to invite *Dan* here tonight! Unless *he* was into aerobics, also?

DAN. At *his* age? Hell, *I* can barely keep up!

MAUVINS. Excuse me, sir, but—perhaps *I* can clear up the mystery somewhat—

DAN. Yes—?

MAUVINS. Well, about a week before he was—was—about a week before he died, Master Josiah had me *telephone* the police department and ask them for a list of *names* of their detective staff. I can only assume Mister *Denton's* name was upon that list.

DAN. Well—yes, it *would* be, of course—but so would a dozen others. Why would he choose me in particular?

MAUVINS. I'm sorry, sir. I haven't the faintest idea.

THEO. Perhaps when the will is read, the mystery will be cleared up?

ELOISE. I certainly *hope* so! I find the present situation utterly baffling! Adler, can't you get *on* with it?!

DAN. (*will sit on* L. *arm of sofa, near LUCRETIA*) Yes, *please*, Mister Sheridan! My curiosity is killing me!

ADLER. No more than my own! I certainly hope *somebody* can clarify matters! (*will leave desk-area and move to chart on* U. *wall*) I want you all to remember that Josiah Travers was a *most* unusual person. Even I, his lawyer, am very much in the dark concerning the nature of his final bequests. I could only carry out his orders—as I am now doing—without so much as a shred of real comprehension as to his aims. (*Has arrived at chart, now; OTHERS have turned in place to be able to see him from wherever they sit.*)

ELOISE. Adler—are you saying that you don't know *who* gets *what*?!

ADLER. (*nods unhappily*) That is *precisely* what I am saying. And now that you are all gathered here together, as Josiah specified, you'll see *why*! (*will grab pull-tab and tug chart down into unrolled position as he says:*) Behold the last will and testament of Josiah Travers! (*See "DETAILS OF WILL-CHART" page.*) Ain't it a beaut?!

(*NOTE: QUINTET at bar will remain seated on stools, but MAUVINS and ZITA will come to their feet, and QUINTET on sofa will stand and move u. for a closer look—ELOISE and THEO moving around R. end of sofa, PIPPI, LUCRETIA and DAN around L. end of sofa; as this latter QUINTET moves u., ZITA and MAUVINS will move a few steps nearer chart, also, but remain in area between phonograph and sofa, and ELOISE/THEO will end up near ADLER slightly to R. of chart, while PIPPI/LUCRETIA/DAN will end up to L. of chart; in other words, we want to preserve* audience *sightlines to chart, but generally move players in a bit closer to it; this movement—of all but ADLER and QUINTET on barstools—will begin as soon as ADLER completes preceding speech, during the following dialogue:*)

ELOISE. What *is* that?!

MAUVINS. Looks like pure gibberish!

THEO. Adler, I don't understand!

BUZZY. Hey, are you *sure* he was of sound mind?!

ADLER. I'm afraid *I* don't know any more about it than *you* do! (*All are by now in their new positions.*)

JERRY. Well, I'll be darned! I might have *guessed* he'd do something like that, the old slyboots!

CONNIE. Jerry! Do you mean you *understand* that thing?

JERRY. Well, not *quite*, of course, but I recognize it for what it *is*!

FLAME. What *is* it?

JERRY. It's a *rebus*!

DAN. A *what*?

JERRY. (*will hop down from stool and move to point between ADLER and chart during his speech*) A *pic-*

ture-puzzle! Those drawings and things stand for *words*. It was one of Josiah's favorite puzzle-forms!

LUCRETIA. Do you mean you can *read* that thing?

PIPPI. What does it *say*?

JERRY. Well, wait, hold it a minute—I can read *some* of it, right off the bat—but other parts will take a little *figuring* . . .

KISSY. Oh! Perhaps *that's* why Jerry was invited tonight! Uncle Josiah *knew* we'd need *someone* to unscramble that mess, and—

DAN. It still doesn't explain why *I* was invited, though . . .

ZITA. I'm sure everything will become clear once we allow Mister Delvin to read it to us!

CONNIE. Zita's right! Go ahead, Jerry—what does it say?!

JERRY. Well, let's see now . . . sometimes certain drawings can have a wide variety of interpretations . . . but I'll make it as clear as it is to *me*, anyhow . . .

THEO. Yes-yes, we quite understand, Jerry.

ELOISE. Just get *to* it!

JERRY. Okay. It begins, "My friends"—

LUCRETIA. We can *see* that!

PIPPI. Don't interrupt, Lu!

JERRY. I *have* to read the *words*, you know, so we can see where the pictures fit in *between* them.

ADLER. Of course you do, my boy. Go right ahead.

JERRY. Thank you. Okay, then: "My friends, Please" —then there's a sort of teddy-bear with the word "me" on its chest, followed by a period—

MAUVINS. Meaning *what*?

JERRY. Well, let's see, now . . . "bear" with "me" on it . . . Oh! That's *it*!

ADLER. *What*?

JERRY. "My friends, Please bear with me," period.

FLAME. Oh, of course! It's *obvious* once you figure it *out*!

ZITA. (*as she and MAUVINS move a bit farther* U. *toward group*) But what can that *next* part mean?

ADLER. Wait a moment — someone should write this down!

KISSY. *I* will! (*Moves to desk, where she will sit, find pen and paper, and will write down explanations as they occur; BUZZY and CONNIE will move there with her, alternating looking up toward chart or — standing on either side of KISSY — watching what she is writing.*)

JERRY. That next part's kind of obscure . . . a pair of rectangles with an arrow indicating the second rectangle, then an ace of clubs . . . the word "whose" . . . then what seems to be a bunch of arms and legs . . .

ELOISE. Oh, dear! That's just like Josiah's *murder*!

ADLER. Eloise, get hold of yourself! The will was written *before* the murder! Josiah could hardly have *known* what was going to happen to him!

THEO. Adler's right, Eloise. Calm down!

JERRY. Shall I go on, or what?

ZITA. Go on, of course!

JERRY. All right . . . then we have the words "enjoy dabbling in re" followed by a couple of buses — *Ah!* Of course!

OTHERS. *What?*

JERRY. It means, "enjoy dabbling in *rebuses*"! See? "In re buses"!

KISSY. Got it! But that stuff that comes *before* it — what do I put down?

CONNIE. (*abruptly elated*) Members!

OTHERS. *What?*

CONNIE. (*excitedly*) Those arms and legs — they're

members! Something about "whose *members* enjoy dabbling in rebuses"! Uncle Josiah used to belong to a club that *specialized* in creating and solving them!

ADLER. *A club!* That's the ace of clubs! "A club whose members enjoyed dabbling in rebuses"!

FLAME. But what can those two *rectangles* mean?

JERRY. That's where rebuses get tough—there are so many varieties of terminology possible. Besides being rectangles, they might also be referred to as boxes, or tetragons, or oblongs—or maybe they're supposed to be two blank sheets of notepaper, end-to-end . . .

PIPPI. But that *arrow* must mean something, doesn't it—?

ELOISE. Pippi, a well-trained parlormaid only speaks when she is spoken to!

THEO. Eloise, under the circumstances, I think propriety should be left by the wayside! Pippi *was* invited, after all—I think Josiah's will should be fair game for *anyone*!

LUCRETIA. Well, then, *I* have a kind of idea . . . (*when OTHERS look her way:*) Whatever those two things are, the arrow seems to mean we should consider only the *second* one, do you see?

PIPPI. *Good* thinking, Lu!

DAN. Yes, that *must* be it! Let's see—"second rectangle a club"—no, that's meaningless.

BUZZY. Well, wait, maybe *that* terminology has its *own* variations. I mean, it could also be "rectangle *number two*, a club"!

KISSY. Or even "*oblong* two"!

JERRY. Kissy, that's *it*! "Oblong two a club"!

ELOISE. I don't *get* it—?!

JERRY. It's a pun! Most rebuses *are*! It means "I belong to a club whose members enjoy dabbling in rebuses"!

ELOISE. (*nearly in tears*) I *still* don't get it—?!

ZITA. "*Ob*long"—"I *belong*"—!

ELOISE. (*suddenly gets it*) *Oh!* Oh, *yes*, of *course!* Why—do you know—this is *fun!*

THEO. Naturally! Why would Josiah have *indulged* in it for all those years if it *wasn't* any fun?!

ADLER. Look, can we please get *on* with it—?!

MAUVINS. *I've* figured the *next* part, right after the comma—that's a sign indicating "therefore"—I remember it from my geometry classes in high school!

JERRY. Good for you, Mauvins!

KISSY. (*has been scribbling furiously*) Got it! What's next?!

JERRY. Oh, this next bit's easy—it was one of the first things I spotted when Mister Sheridan rolled down the chart. In the midst of all those words, we have a drawing of an open tin can . . . a mustachioed balding man with an Elizabethan ruff around his neck . . . and what must be a Bible, just before the next period. Figure the man to be William Shakespeare—I mean, *he's* certainly Elizabethan, and the sketch looks like a painting of him I saw once—

ELOISE. But what could "my last Shakespeare" possibly mean?!

JERRY. Not "Shakespeare"—"Will"!

ADLER. (*with awed realization*) Of course! So this next part means—"therefore I have decided to leave my vast fortune to anyone—friend, relative or stranger—who can decode this, my last will and—uh—and—"?

PIPPI. *Testament!*

(*OTHERS variously babble* "Yes!", "Of course!", "That *must* be it!" *and similar ad-libs for a moment; then:*)

JERRY. I'm afraid I'm stymied by that *next* drawing, though. Looks like someone machine-gunned a pair of salamis! Anyone else care to give it a try?

ELOISE. (*getting into the spirit of things*) Let's see . . . "holy sausages"!

BUZZY. That sounds like a line from *Batman and Robin*!

MAUVINS. "Perforated pepperoni"?

ZITA. That *alliterates* nicely—but what *sense* does it make?

LUCRETIA. Actually, those things look more like *hot dogs* to me . . . but what could "punctured hot dogs" mean?

JERRY. Look, let's skip that one and move on. Maybe it'll make sense to us once we know the *context*!

DAN. What *picture* are we supposed to look behind?

KISSY. (*swivels a bit, points up at* R. *wall*) *That's* the only one in the *room* . . .

BUZZY. So what's *behind* it? (*will start to lift picture*)

ADLER. (*even as BUZZY exposes it:*) Josiah's wall safe! It's location was *supposed* to be a *secret*!

CONNIE. Oh, Adler, don't get huffy! Uncle Josiah obviously *wanted* us to see it, or why put it into the *will*?

FLAME. But whose *faces* are those *in* the picture?

KISSY. Well, on the left, that's Sandra Dee, the movie actress . . .

BUZZY. And some kind of animal's paw with a *whopper* of a *pimple* on it . . .

JERRY. (*has moved down to stand just* U. *of desk, with OTHERS—those persons not already at desk—following him*) And that guy on the right is Johann Sebastian Bach, if I remember rightly . . . but who's the gal cheek-to-cheek with him?

MAUVINS. Seems to me she's another movie actress . . . the face is very familiar . . .

PIPPI. Barbara Bach! Of course!

ADLER. Right next to Johann Sebastian Bach! The name-similarity must *mean* something!

ELOISE. Let's add it all up, and see what we've got!

THEO. A wall safe—

LUCRETIA. Sandra Dee—

KISSY. A paw with a big *zit* on it—

THEO. Barbara Bach—

CONNIE. And Johann Sebastian Bach—!

DAN. Hell, *that* doesn't add up to *anything*!

FLAME. But it *must*! Otherwise, why would Josie have *indicated* it?!

ZITA. I've *got* it!

OTHERS. *What?*

ZITA. (*enumerating on fingers:*) A wall safe—Sandra Dee—a paw with a zit—and a pair of Bachs!

(*Laid out like this, it becomes obvious to the next four speakers, who shout with increasing excitement:*)

JERRY. Safe—!

CONNIE. Dee—!

BUZZY. Paw zit—!

KISSY. Bachs!

ALL. *Safe deposit box!*

JERRY. (*rushes back to chart, OTHERS—except CONNIE, BUZZY and KISSY—following him in an eager scramble*) "You will find a large sum of—" whatever those ventilated wienies mean! "in a safe deposit box in . . . in . . ." (*sags, despondent*) A wobbly vase?

FLAME. Buzzy's nurse! She phoned about a broken vase—?!

BUZZY. Flame, use your head — how could Josiah Travers have known that my nurse would get butterfingered the night the will was read?!

FLAME. (*slumps, disappointed*) Well — that's true enough, I guess . . .

BUZZY. Of course, that silly urn has been *loose* for awhile, just about *ready* to take a tumble — but *Josiah* wouldn't know about it . . .

JERRY. Buzzy, that's *it*!

OTHERS. *What?*

JERRY. The sketch doesn't mean a wobbly vase . . . it means a *loose urn*!

ADLER. Of course! It makes perfect sense, now!

ELOISE. (*weepy with frustration*) Not to *me* it doesn't!

DAN. (*just catching on*) Loose urn! — *Lucerne*! The town in Switzerland!

THEO. But — why go all the way to Lucerne in Switzerland to fill a safe deposit box with porous bratwurst?!

JERRY. (*shrugs*) We'll just *have* to let that part *go* for awhile. Let's move on.

PIPPI. What's that written on that hypodermic?

ELOISE. "Procaine." A kind of local anesthetic.

LUCRETIA. That stuff the dentist pumps into your gums before he starts drilling, Pippi.

PIPPI. Oh, *that* stuff! I hate the way it makes you feel — !

MAUVINS. On the contrary, you mean the way it makes you *not* feel. Everything goes totally numb.

KISSY. Not as numb as you'd *like* it to be, though. I can *still* feel the drilling a little.

CONNIE. You should *tell* the dentist when that happens, Kissy, so he'll give you a little *more*!

PIPPI. Oh, no! Bad enough feeling *numb*, without feeling even *number*!

JERRY. That's *it*! It's another *pun*! Procaine is a number! (*pronounces it "NUM-r"*) But if you write it out, it's spelled exactly like "number"! (*pronounces it "NUM-ber"*)

ELOISE. The number of the safe deposit box in Lucerne! (*unwontedly claps her hands and does a little dance*) Oh, this is more fun all the time! (*sees OTHERS all staring at her in surprise, freezes*) With—with all due respect to the dear departed, of course . . .

THEO. Come off it, Eloise, you're enjoying yourself immensely! Why not admit it?

ELOISE. Well—perhaps a *tiny* bit . . .

KISSY. Are we taking a dance-break, or what? 'Cause if we are, I want another drink!

ADLER. No, of course we're not! Mister Delvin, would you please continue?

JERRY. I don't know if I *can*—I mean, the significance of that empty mailbox eludes me completely . . .

LUCRETIA. Let's try it in context—(*reads carefully from the chart:*) ". . . you will find a large sum of"—whatever those sausages mean—"in a safe deposit box in Lucerne, the number of which is first, initially, the"—something—"of this group . . ."

ZITA. *That's* odd!

THEO. *What's* odd, Zita?

ZITA. Why would Josiah say "first" *and* "initially"? They both mean the same thing, don't they?

CONNIE. It must be some kind of *clue*!

JERRY. Yeah, a puzzle-lover like Josiah wouldn't make a mistake like that . . .

BUZZY. Of course, he was expecting a meat-cleaver at any moment—!

PIPPI. That can't be!

MAUVINS. Pippi is quite correct—the will was com-

pleted *long* before Master Josiah was—that is, before
somebody—well—

ADLER. Yes, the will was completed at least a week
before his death—maybe even *two* weeks—I forget exactly—I'll have to look it up.

FLAME. But what about the empty mailbox?!

DAN. Yes, we're getting off the track! Does anyone
have any ideas?

ELOISE. (*less and less sedate, as excitement grips her*)
Let's be logical: An empty mailbox means there's no
mail . . .

KISSY. Could it refer to a postal holiday?

ADLER. (*looks at chart, tries it*) ". . . the postal holiday of this group . . ." Makes no sense at all.

FLAME. Maybe it's the *name* of the holiday? Like
Christmas—?

BUZZY. President's Day—?

PIPPI. Memorial Day—?

LUCRETIA. Labor Day—?

JERRY. No, they don't seem to make any sense at
all . . .

THEO. Maybe a *semi*-holiday, like Halloween?

ZITA. Halloween's not a holiday at *all*!

BUZZY. It is in *Transylvania*. . . !

MAUVINS. (*looking quite bemused*) I *wonder*, now—!

OTHERS. *What?*

MAUVINS. Well, I was *born* on Halloween, but—I
can't seem to fit my birthday into the text—" . . . the
Mauvins' birthday of this group . . ."

BUZZY. Hey! Maybe *that's* what the *sausages* mean!

OTHERS. *What?*

BUZZY. Halloween!

JERRY. How do you *figure*, Buzzy?

BUZZY. (*gives a what*-else? *shrug, on:*) Hollow wienies!

KISSY. Oh, come *on*, Buzzy!

BUZZY. Hell, it's as good as anything *else* we've thought of —!

CONNIE. Buzzy's got a *point* —

ELOISE. (*irritably*) *Maybe* on the top of his *head*!

DAN. Now, stop that! Let's do this thing calmly, shall we?

ELOISE. (*sighs*) All right, all right. Sorry, Doctor Burdett.

BUZZY. Forget it. We're *all* kind of tense right now.

JERRY. (*who has been scowling at chart, suddenly brightens*) Letters! *That's* it! An empty mailbox means "missing letters"!

CONNIE. Jerry, honey, *that* can't be right — I mean, we're looking for *numbers*, not *letters* . . . right?

JERRY. (*reluctantly*) Well — yeah, I guess you're right . . .

ADLER. Let's move on to the next clue. We can always backtrack later.

ZITA. Good idea. What can the significance of that guy in the *toga* be?

BUZZY. And why is he pushing a *teapot* away?

KISSY. A teapot wearing a *beret*!

ELOISE. And don't forget the *plus*-sign right in front of the guy!

PIPPI. Could that guy be Julius Caesar? I mean, *he* used to wear one of those coral reefs around his head —!

LUCRETIA. "Laurel wreaths"!

PIPPI. Whatever!

JERRY. Caesar! Of course! And what *was* his final word?

FLAME. Didn't he say, "*Et tu, Brute*"?

DAN. He did in the *play*, I know — but did he in *real* life?

THEO. Yes! I remember that from school. Shakespeare was using an actual quote at that point — that's why he left it in Latin!

MAUVINS. But what's *that* got to do with a beret and a teapot?

FLAME. Maybe it's a *French* teapot!

KISSY. What's French for "teapot"?

PIPPI. Search *me*!

ADLER. The French word for "tea" is "thè" . . . is *that* any help? (*NOTE: "thè" is pronounced "tay."*)

JERRY. Wait a minute . . . "*Et tu, Brute*" . . . "*brew thè*"! Brewing tea! But get *rid* of that part — !

BUZZY. That leaves "*Et tu*" . . . But where does that leave *us*?

ELOISE. (*elated*) "*Et tu*"! Those are *numbers*! Eight . . . two. . . !

DAN. But it's not *enough*! I'm *sure* the number of a safe deposit box in Switzerland would be longer than *that*. . . !

THEO. Maybe that's what the *plus*-sign means!

FLAME. Of course! Those are only the *last two* numbers! That empty mailbox must indicate the numbers that come *before* them!

KISSY. But how? What do missing letters have to do with numbers?

LUCRETIA. Why don't we go *on*, and come back to that part later?

CONNIE. Yes, why *don't* we!

MAUVINS. Fine by *me*!

ZITA. What *is* that next drawing, anyhow?

KISSY. Seems obvious to me — it's a sailor lying in the sun.

ZITA. No, I mean that thing down by his feet!

BUZZY. Looks like a squashed football.

CONNIE. Or a badly drawn valentine-heart . . .

ELOISE. *I* think it's a *kidney*!

LUCRETIA. You're *all* wrong! It's a bean! I'm a cook — trust me!

JERRY. Hey, I think she's right!

THEO. A *navy* bean! It has to be! Otherwise, why draw that sailor?

PIPPI. No, it's too flat for that — more like a *lima* bean . . .

ADLER. Hold it! I don't think it's the *kind* of bean at *all*! I think it simply means *bean*! — That makes the phrase read, "P.S. You should also know that I have *been* —" (*pronounces it "bean" rather than "bin"*)

FLAME. That he has been *what*? Been given a tanning by a sailor?!

MAUVINS. Why don't we come back to *that* one later, too.

DAN. That *next* one's *really* puzzling!

KISSY. The speed-limit sign? What's so hard to figure? "Zero-zero miles per hour" — seems simple enough to *me*!

DAN. But why *two* zeros? "*Zero* miles per hour" would mean the same thing!

JERRY. Dan's right. That double-zero must be significant, somehow!

BUZZY. Roulette! That's the only thing *I* know that uses a double-zero!

THEO. Do you suppose it refers to Las Vegas?

ZITA. Might also be Monte Carlo!

CONNIE. Or even Atlantic City!

JERRY. Which means it probably doesn't refer to *any* of them! A clue *that* vague wouldn't be playing fair!

MAUVINS. Why don't we get on to the *last* sketch, and then we can go *back* over everything.

PIPPI. Let's see — there's a diamond marked "A.D."

and another diamond marked "B.C." — and the second one is stuck in that *eye*!

LUCRETIA. (*musing aloud*) Diamond . . . diamond-in-eye . . . *old* diamond-in-eye . . .

JERRY. *Gem!* Not diamond! It's a *horoscope* sign! *Gem*-in-eye!

ELOISE. But *Josiah* wasn't into horoscopes — ! (*then, less certainly, to THEO*) Was he?

THEO. No, of course he wasn't.

BUZZY. But why *two* diamonds?

KISSY. *Older!* The first diamond is just a setup, showing a gem that's of *recent* age, so we'll know the other one is *older*!

JERRY. Of course! So the last part reads: ". . . an older gemini in this very house. Kindly *see to*" — at least, that "C" and "two" seem to be as simple as that — "Kindly see to the usual legalities inherent in such instances."

DAN. In *what* instances?

ADLER. Listen! As the lawyer in the group, that "legalities" part must somehow refer to *me*, don't you agree?

MAUVINS. That would *seem* to make sense . . .

ELOISE. But where does all this *leave* us?

JERRY. Kissy — what have you *got*, so far?

KISSY. (*sighs*) Not a lot, I'm afraid. Here's what it says, more or less — (*reads from paper she's been scribbling on:*) "My friends, Please bear with me. I belong to a club whose members enjoy dabbling in rebuses, therefore I have decided to leave my vast fortune to anyone — friend, relative, or stranger — who can decode this, my last will and testament — "

ELOISE. *What?!* Do you mean to say — there won't be

any specific bequests?!

THEO. It would certainly *seem* so, dear . . .

ELOISE. But—that's not *fair!*

CONNIE. It was *Uncle Josiah's* money, Aunt Eloise—he should be able to dispose of it in any way he wanted.

ELOISE. Easy for *you* to say! He's *already* set up trust funds for you and Kirsten and Theodosia—!

JERRY. Look, you can fight it out later about the terms of the will. Let's try to see what those terms *are*, first, shall we?

DAN. Jerry's right. Go ahead, Kissy.

KISSY. Okay—but here's where it starts getting kind of murky . . . (*reads:*) "You will find a large sum of"—perforated hot dogs— "in a safe deposit box in Lucerne, the number of which is first, initially, the"—that empty mailbox—"of this group, plus eight-two. Good luck to you all!" Signed, "Josiah Travers." Then, "P.S.: You should also know that I have been"—that sailor in the sun—"by zero-zero miles per hour, an older gemini in this very house. Kindly see to the usual legalities inherent in such instances." And then his initials after the P.S. And that's it.

MAUVINS. (*thoughtfully*) Gemini . . . gemini . . . I wonder if—?

ADLER. Look, let's get *all* those drawings solved before we try to figure anything *else* out, *okay*?

FLAME. Maybe we should break for dinner, and come back to it!

ELOISE. I thought you had a Big Mac on the way over?

FLAME. Yeah, but the drinking has given me an appetite!

LUCRETIA. (*moves kitchenward*) Come on, Pippi, you can help me slice the roast!

PIPPI. Sure thing! (*They will exit* D.R. *during:*)

THEO. (*moves toward archway*) The dining room is this way . . .

ELOISE. (*tagging after her*) I still think the whole thing is damnably unfair —!

ADLER. (*moving after ELOISE*) Now-now, Eloise, we don't *know* that — not yet — not till the *entire* will is figured out . . . (*Trio will exit* R. *after passing* U. *through archway.*)

JERRY. I *wish* I could figure out that empty-mailbox thing. . . !

BUZZY. It's those *frankfurters* with the *holes* that are driving *me* nuts!

(*JERRY will move to stand directly before chart, just staring at it and pondering; FLAME, DAN, KISSY, BUZZY and CONNIE will meander to the bar and each fix a drink — or one of them can fix drinks for all — while ZITA stands in area between closet and sofa, eyes closed, fingertips to temples, concentrating, and MAUVINS hovers uncertainly, midway between JERRY and ZITA.*)

JERRY. (*pondering aloud*) Missing letters . . . first missing letters . . . first *initially* missing letters. . . !

FLAME. Shouldn't we be asking around to find out which one of the group is a *gemini*?

BUZZY. But what would a person's *birth-date* have to do with anything?

CONNIE. Maybe it would become clear once we *knew* who it was —?

ZITA. (*still in same pose*) Evil! There is evil here! I feel it! It is very nearby . . . and coming nearer. . . !

DAN. Is she kidding?!

KISSY. Don't scoff, Dan. Zita has some *very* unusual gifts!

FLAME. Look, *puzzling* is bad enough — let's not move on to *spooky*!

DAN. There *is* a kind of creepy feeling in the air, *isn't* there! We need a change of atmosphere — Mauvins, why don't you put some records on — ?

MAUVINS. (*glad of being given something to do*) As you wish, Lieutenant Denton . . . (*will move to phonograph, start sorting through the stack of records there*)

JERRY. (*galvanized*) Initials! First initials! *That's* why Josiah used *both* words! And I think it even explains *Dan*!

DAN. What are you talking about?

JERRY. (*excitedly, joins group at bar*) You said you'd never met him — and yet Josiah selected *you* to be here tonight — *after* he checked out the names of *all* the detectives in your department. It must be because your name begins with a "D"! What other reason could there be?

KISSY. But why send for a *detective* at *all*?!

ZITA. Because of the *evil*! (*will move toward group at bar, now, as she continues:*) I *knew* there was something in the air! I think that, somewhere in that will — Josiah was giving us a clue to his *killer*!

CONNIE. Yipe! I wish that didn't make sense!

JERRY. Those letters — our initials — what *are* they? Let's see — taking them alphabetically —

KISSY. (*hurrying back to desk*) I'd better put them down on paper — !

BUZZY. (*moving after her*) Good idea!

FLAME. (*still at bar with JERRY, ZITA and DAN*) But *which* initial? I mean, *my* name and *Dan's* and *Buzzy's* are the *same*, first *or* last, but — ?

JERRY. No-no, Josiah said "*first* initially"! It *must* be the *first* name.

KISSY. (*scribbling on new sheet of paper*) Hold on, I've nearly got it . . . How's this—?! (*reads:*) "Adler, Buzzy, Connie, Dan, Eloise, Flame" . . . then there's no G, H or I . . . then "Jerry, myself—Kissy—Lucretia" . . . then we skip to "Pippi" . . . then another skip to "Theodosia" . . . and we end with "Zita"!

BUZZY. (*who has been finger-counting*) Wait, that's only twelve names. You left somebody out.

CONNIE. (*scanning list*) It *seems* to be complete . . . who did we—?

FLAME. Mauvins!

MAUVINS. (*turns from records, facing toward desk*) Yes, ma'am?

KISSY. Oh, of course! I meant to stop at his name and ask him, and then I was so busy alphabetizing that I forgot.

JERRY. (*as he, ZITA, and FLAME move deskward*) Forgot to ask him *what*?

(*Unnoticed by anyone, closet door eases open slightly, and a black-gloved hand gropes for lightswitch #3.*)

KISSY. His *first name*, of course!

MAUVINS. Begging your pardon, ma'am, but—Mauvins *is* my first name.

JERRY. Isn't that unusual? I thought butlers always went by *last* names?

MAUVINS. That is so, Mister Delvin, but Master Josiah was most insistent about calling me by my first name—he said something about, um, if I wanted to be mentioned in his *will*—do you see?

BUZZY. The will?! Hey, then the names *really* must be a clue!

CONNIE. And what *is* your last name, Mauvins?

MAUVINS. Why, it's—

(*Then the gloved hand flicks lightswitch #3, and LIGHTS GO OUT; in darkness, women SCREAM, and:*)

JERRY. What happened?

DAN. Somebody turned out the lights!

BUZZY. There's a switch by the door, here, if I can *find* it—! Ah, *there* it is!

(*LIGHTS COME UP FULL; BUZZY is at lightswitch #1; rest of group at desk is still in approximately same positions we last saw them; and MAUVINS is lying face down on floor—feet near phonograph, parallel to proscenium—with the handle of a dagger in the middle of his back; OTHERS react, then rush toward him, during:*)

CONNIE. Mauvins!

KISSY. He's been stabbed!

ZITA. I *knew* I felt the approach of evil!

BUZZY. Too bad *Mauvins* didn't!

JERRY. (*first to arrive, checks MAUVINS' pulse*) I think he's *dead*!

DAN. But—*how*? There was nobody anywhere *near* him!

CONNIE. But why would anybody want to kill *Mauvins*?

KISSY. Who could *do* such a thing?

JERRY. And *how* did they do it?

ZITA. Yes, from whence did the hand of evil *descend*?
BUZZY. Well, *one* thing we all know for *sure*!
OTHERS. *What?*
BUZZY. (*points to fallen body*) The *butler* didn't do it! (*and, as all remain frozen, staring down at corpse—*)

THE CURTAIN FALLS

End of Act One

Several hours later, about midnight the same day.
Curtain-rise finds PIPPI, on hands and knees, just
    completing scrubbing — via scrub-brush and bucket —
    the floor-area where MAUVINS had lain (if your
    stage has carpeting, then she can just be completing
    vacuuming the same area); our "drinkers" — FLAME,
    JERRY, BUZZY, CONNIE and KISSY — are on the
    barstools again, each with a drink in hand; AD-
    LER, his back to us, stand directly before chart,
    pondering; ZITA is seated at center of sofa, head
    back, eyes shut, arms crossed upon her chest, look-
    ing almost trance-like; a moment after curtain-rise,
    LUCRETIA peeks in through kitchen door.

LUCRETIA. Aren't you finished *yet*? I need a hand
with the dishes!

PIPPI. (*drops brush into bucket — or turns off and un-*
plugs vacuum — outlet could be near baseboard under
lightswitch #3) Sorry, Lu. Those chalk-marks don't
come up very easily! (*She will take — whatever — equip-*
ment toward kitchen, and LUCRETIA will remain there
long enough to hold door open to facilitate her exit,
then both will exit into kitchen, during:)

BUZZY. Why do the police always draw chalk-marks
around a body?

KISSY. So they can take photographs of the spot, I
think, and know where it *was*.

CONNIE. Why not just photograph the *body*?

FLAME. They *did* photograph the body!

JERRY. Then why bother with the chalk-marks at *all*?

CONNIE. Maybe they just like making messes!

FLAME. I wonder what's keeping Dan? He promised
he'd come right back.

ADLER. (*distracted from his pondering, moves to bar,*

now) Probably paperwork. Policemen spend *most* of their time doing paperwork. (*will go behind bar and fix drink, during:*)

JERRY. We should count ourselves lucky we *had* a police detective on the premises when the murder occurred! Our story of *how* it happened would have sounded *fantastic*!

BUZZY. What gets *me* is—just how *did* it happen?

FLAME. What do you mean, Buzzy?

KISSY. Seems simple enough to *me* . . .

CONNIE. Me, too! The lights went out—and somebody stabbed him!

BUZZY. Yeah, but those lights weren't out more than five seconds! How could anybody *get* to him, *do* the deed, and then get *away* in that short a time?

ADLER. Perhaps the killer was wearing *track* shoes!

JERRY. (*will set drink on bar, and move* D.L., *during:*) It really *is* baffling, though, Adler . . . (*CONNIE will trail after him, curious, while ADLER moves down with his drink and sits at desk.*)

ADLER. Sometimes one's sense of time gets distorted under stress. The interval of darkness may have been *much* longer—in fact, it would almost *have* to be, since our killer obviously *did* arrive, do the poor man in, and depart, without anyone seeing him—or her!

FLAME. I *wish* you wouldn't call him "our" killer, Adler! It makes me feel like I'm on his *waiting*-list!

ADLER. Nonsense! Why would the killer want to go after *you*?

KISSY. Why did he want to go after *Mauvins*?!

BUZZY. Well, wait, now—Mauvins was just about to *tell* us something when he got it—probably something that would *betray* the killer somehow.

CONNIE. (*over near phonograph with JERRY, now,*

looks his way) But Buzzy, the killer *wasn't* a killer *yet*!

FLAME. We can't *know* that! I mean — after all — *some-body* killed your great-uncle *Josiah*!

JERRY. But if Mauvins *knew* who'd done it, why didn't he tell the *police*?

ADLER. Perhaps he didn't *realize* what he knew — that is, didn't realize it had anything to *do* with Josiah's death until —

KISSY. Until *what*?

ADLER. (*shrugs*) Who knows? Whatever he was about to say, it died when he did. (*takes large swallow of drink*) *I* certainly can't imagine what he was planning to tell us!

JERRY. We don't *have* to imagine, Adler! We *know*!

CONNIE. We *do*?

JERRY. He was *about* to tell us his *last name*!

CONNIE. But what significance could his *name* have?

JERRY. If we knew *that*, we might be able to expose our *killer*!

FLAME. "*The*" killer, *please*?!

JERRY. Sorry.

FLAME. (*leaves bar area, will move toward* D.L.) Oh, what's keeping Dan, anyhow?!

BUZZY. (*will follow after her*) What's *with* you and Dan, Flame? You two weren't into more than aerobics, were you?

FLAME. (*turns to face him*) Of *course* not! (*then, less vociferously*) That is — well, we *did* go out to *dinner* a few times after class . . .

BUZZY. Didn't that defeat the purpose of all your exercise?

FLAME. Aerobics always gives me an appetite!

JERRY. But why *are* you so concerned about Dan's return?

FLAME. (*will continue on down to JERRY and CON-NIE, now, with BUZZY tagging after her*) Because I want to go home! And Dan said none of us were to go anywhere until he got back! Is that so unreasonable?

CONNIE. I hope he's not going to *question* us! *I* get nervous enough taking pop-quizzes in the *newspaper*!

ADLER. An innocent person has nothing to fear, Connie.

BUZZY. (*to ADLER*) Have you strolled through *Central Park* lately?

ADLER. I mean from the police!

BUZZY. Then what do the station-houses *do* with all those rubber hoses? (*As ADLER fumes and disdains replying, BUZZY focuses on ZITA, who has been motionless since curtain-rise.*) You know, if she sits that way much longer, a couple of Egyptians are going to tiptoe in and clap her into a mummy-case!

ZITA. (*breaks stance, scowls at him*) Do not mock what you do not understand, Doctor Burdett!

CONNIE. But Zita—what *are* you meditating about, anyhow?

ZITA. I am trying to find the focal point of the evil aura in this house!

JERRY. Any luck?

ZITA. Not so far. But there is something—a flicker—a glimmering—!

ADLER. But would it hold up in a court of law?

ZITA. (*snaps her fingers in contempt*) The law! Bah! It knows *nothing* of the infinite—of the horrible throbbing emanations that pure evil gives off! Only *I* can sense such things!

BUZZY. But if the law won't believe you, what good does it do?

ZITA. (*shrugs*) Once I *know* who the killer is, I can *in-*

form the authorities, and they can pinpoint their *investigation* of that person!

KISSY. But what if that doesn't *help*? I mean, if the investigation can't turn up anything illegal about the person — all you've done is let a *killer* know that you're *onto* him!

FLAME. And *that's* not what *I* call very bright!

ZITA. Pah! If the *law* will do nothing, why — then *I* will do something!

JERRY. Whoa, there! That could be mighty dangerous!

CONNIE. Stalking a forewarned killer — !

ZITA. (*stands, folds arms regally*) I, Zita Van Zok, will not *have* to stalk! No murderer, no matter *how* strong-willed, can resist the full brunt of *my* powers!

BUZZY. Come off it, Zita! I don't believe in sorcery!

ZITA. (*turns, points finger at him, eyes flashing*) You are an *idiot*!

BUZZY. (*will* instantly *lurch about, eyes crossed, tongue lolling, and utter the words:*) Guh-DOY, guh-DOY, guh-DOY — !

ZITA. (*instantly apologetic*) Oops! Sorry about that! (*snaps fingers*) Return to normal!

BUZZY. (*straightens, dazed, looks about*) Where am I? What happened? What did she — ?

JERRY. Holy Toledo, Zita, what the hell did you *do* to him?!

CONNIE. Jerry, I *told* you she had strange powers!

FLAME. This is fascinating! Oh, Zita, you *must* come and do your stuff for my kindergarten class! The kids would go crazy for you!

ZITA. Really, Miss Fondue, my powers are not a *toy*!

FLAME. I only thought —

ZITA. (*as THEO descends stairs into view*) My dear,

all I meant was that I—well—do *not* do *conjuring* tricks! My powers are very *real*! The children could become terribly frightened by a demonstration!

BUZZY. Then you don't know *kids* very well, Zita! They're probably the most bloodthirsty little—well—let's say that blood and gore are—to borrow from *The Sound of Music*—"some of their favorite things!"

THEO. (*unnoticed till she speaks*) Did I *miss* anything, my dears? (*OTHERS now look her way.*)

CONNIE. Buzzy just got an accidental dose of Zita's *whammy*-power.

KISSY. Otherwise, it's been Dullsville all the way! How's Eloise?

THEO. Finally asleep. Luckily, I had some sedatives in the medicine cabinet. The poor dear was almost *hysterical* about Mauvins' murder. (*will move to join KISSY at bar, but not make a drink*)

BUZZY. *I* wasn't exactly the picture of serenity, *myself*! I mean, here we are, casually chatting—and all at once, darkness, screaming, and lights come up on an unexpected corpse! *Brrrr!*

THEO. Has anyone figured out what happened, exactly?

JERRY. That's what we were *trying* to do, just before that whammy. (*looks about at phonograph*) Frankly, I'm baffled! There's *no* way a killer could have come and gone in that short space of time—but it happened!

KISSY. Well, at least we know who *didn't* do it!

THEO. What do you mean, dear?

KISSY. Well, it *wasn't* anyone in the bunch of us over by the *desk*—!

ADLER. You can't be *certain* of that, Kissy—in the darkness, well—

KISSY. Listen, even an Olympic *medalist* couldn't have galloped across this entire room, killed Mauvins, and galloped back to join us before Buzzy turned the lights on again! For *one* thing, we'd have *heard* him!

JERRY. Hey, that's right! We didn't hear *anything*— not a *footstep*—during the time the lights were out!

CONNIE. Of course, we ladies were *screaming* pretty loudly . . .

JERRY. Yeah, but running footsteps are an entirely different *kind* of noise—you don't just hear them—you feel them through the feet! And I'll swear there wasn't so much as a *rustle* of sound like that!

THEO. Really, now, *how* it was done is less relevant than the fact that it *was* done! And until we know by *whom* . . . the nightmare goes on!

ADLER. It's no *wonder* poor Eloise is upset!

THEO. I wish the murder was *all* she was upset about!

KISSY. What *else* is there?

THEO. I'm afraid she's even *more* disturbed about— Jerry Delvin!

JERRY. About *me*?

CONNIE. Oh, dear, I *knew* we should have told her about the engagement!

THEO. My dear, it has nothing to *do* with your *engagement* to Jerry. It has to do, rather, with his line of *work*—!

BUZZY. That's not fair! So, okay, he doesn't make the big bucks suitable to a marriage into the social register, but—

THEO. I'm afraid you're all missing my point.

ZITA. You mean missing *Eloise's* point . . . don't you?

THEO. (*thoughtfully*) I'm . . . not sure.

JERRY. (*his back up slightly*) Just what are you getting at, Mrs. Travers?

THEO. Well, after all, Jerry—you *are* a puzzle expert — and the unusual form of Josiah's will *does* require specialized knowledge to interpret.

JERRY. (*very much at sea*) . . . *And*. . . ?

THEO. Eloise wondered . . . and got *me* wondering as well . . . how can I put this delicately — ?

JERRY. If you're trying to spare my feelings, it's a bit too late!

CONNIE. Jerry!

THEO. Actually, it was *Connie's* feelings I was concerned about.

KISSY. What *are* you trying to *say*?!

THEO. Just this: How do we *know* that we can *trust* Jerry's interpretation of the will?

ADLER. (*rises slowly*) I — I never *thought* of that — ! (*to JERRY*) How *do* we know you're not hoaxing the *lot* of us, sir?!

JERRY. You're being ridiculous! *Why* should I —

THEO. Josiah left a lot of money. Why *shouldn't* you?

BUZZY. Hold it, everybody! Use your heads! If Jerry came up with the *wrong* number on that safe deposit box in Lucerne, we'd find out the minute we tried to look it up!

ZITA. There is *other* information in that will, Doctor Burdett — such as the identity of Josiah's murderer!

ADLER. What are you talking about?!

ZITA. A clever man — a man like Josiah — suspecting he was about to be killed — would find some way of leaving a message — I rather think that the *postscript* is the part containing the vital information . . .

KISSY. Honestly, Zita, you can't expect us to believe Uncle was killed by a *sailor*!

CONNIE. Or a speed-limit sign, for that matter!

FLAME. But how about that *gemini*? I seem to remember Mauvins getting *very* bemused the moment *that* part was solved — !

THEO. But I've already *told* you that Josiah wasn't *into* horoscopes!

JERRY. Then—what if it means something *else*?!

BUZZY. Like a *real* diamond in somebody's eye?

JERRY. No-no, what *I* meant was—

(*Then all react as a LOUD SCREAM sounds, distantly.*)

THEO. That sounded like Eloise! (*starts for archway, OTHERS following*)

CONNIE. I thought you said she was heavily sedated?!

KISSY. With a *killer* on the loose, how could *anyone* get to sleep?!

(*By now, all have exited through archway and up stairs; an instant later, LUCRETIA rushes in from kitchen, headed straight for closet, with a tearful PIPPI in her wake, on:*)

LUCRETIA. Good, they're gone! I'm getting *out* of here!

PIPPI. But the *police*, Lu! That detective said nobody was to leave!

LUCRETIA. If you have any brains, *you'll* leave, *too*, girl! A killer can only be fried *once*! What's *another* murder more-or-less?!

PIPPI. But the police will go after you—they'll find you—and—!

LUCRETIA. (*vanishing into closet*) By the time they know I'm gone, I'll already be on a plane to Switzerland!

PIPPI. Lu! You've figured out the will!

LUCRETIA. (*comes out of closet, slipping into top-coat*) Of course I have! *All* of it! *Including* the name of the *killer*! (*suddenly thoughtful, moves* D. *a few steps*)

And listen — Pippi — if anything should happen to me —
well — you and I have been good friends a long time, and
I don't have very much in the way of possessions, but —
(*indicates stuffed bird behind chair*) I'd like you to have
this — *if* anything goes wrong — if only as a momento —
it certainly can't be *worth* very much — !

PIPPI. Lu, don't *talk* like that! Don't go, please! If
you know who the killer is, you should *tell* somebody!

LUCRETIA. *After* I collect those Swiss francs — for the
two of us!

PIPPI. *What* Swiss francs?

LUCRETIA. (*moving toward archway, waves toward
chart*) Those *hot dogs* with the *holes* in them! What *else*
could they mean?! Now, if you'll excuse me, I'm in a
hurry! (*PIPPI will follow her u. through archway.*)
And not a *word*, now, to *anyone*, do you understand? If
the killer thinks *you* might know what *I* know, you'd be
in terrible danger!

PIPPI. But Lu — are you *sure* you figured out the number of that safe deposit box correctly?

LUCRETIA. Easy as pie! Just list all the first names
alphabetically, and add up the totals of the *missing* letters of the alphabet, group by group! Be careful, honey.
I've got to go!

PIPPI. (*grabs her arm before she can open front door*)
Lu! Please! Tell *me* who the killer is! At least I'll know
who to steer clear of — !

LUCRETIA. But I don't have *time* to explain how I
figured out —

PIPPI. *Skip* that part! Just give me the *name*! (*DOOR
CHIMES SOUND; both react.*) It's that detective, back
already!

LUCRETIA. (*dashing toward closet, with its still-open
door*) He mustn't know I've gone! Not a word to any-

one! I'll sneak out as soon as there's nobody around!
(*hurries into closet, shuts door*)

PIPPI. (*almost sobbing*) But what if he has to hang up
his *coat*—?! (*stands irresolute, still in front hall, wring-
ing hands; then, from somewhere on stairs, we hear:*)

CONNIE. Pippi, why aren't you getting the door?
(*PIPPI rushes to do so, admitting DAN, as CONNIE,
ADLER, FLAME, KISSY, JERRY and BUZZY de-
scend into hall.*)

DAN. (*doffing topcoat*) I'm sorry I kept you all
waiting so long, but—well—I had a lot of information
to get hold of. (*will move toward closet, OTHERS following him*) Where's Miss Ainsley and that Van Zok
woman? (*looks at group, adds:*) *And* Mrs. Travers?

PIPPI. (*taking advantage of his semi-turned head,
takes coat from over his arm, deftly*) Here, sir, let me
hang that up for you!

DAN. What—? Oh, really, Pippi, there's no need to—

PIPPI. Then I'll just put it on the chair, if that's all
right? (*She will drape coat over back of armchair, during:*)

DAN. Yes, that will be fine, Pippi, thank you!

FLAME. Is this going to take very long, Lieutenant
Denton? The sooner I'm safe home in my own bed, the
happier I'll be.

DAN. That all depends on how quickly I can get some
truthful answers. Would you all please find seats?

(*Over next speeches, seating will be as follows: PIPPI
on front lip of armchair cushion, just U. of footstool; ADLER returns to drink he left on desk, and
sits on front edge of desk; FLAME and KISSY sit
side-by-side on barstools; and BUZZY will remain
standing, but leaning on elbow on U. end of bar,*)

while JERRY and CONNIE settle on sofa, twisted partway to look toward DAN, who stands in area between chart and sofa; even while they are moving into place:)

ADLER. In answer to your earlier question, Lieutenant, Theo and Zita are seeing to Eloise, upstairs. She had a rather bad scare, and when she screamed, we all ran up there. That's where we were returning from when you arrived.

DAN. Scare? What sort of scare?

CONNIE. It was *nothing*, really. She woke up in a semi-dark room, and there was a lounging-robe thrown carelessly over a chair beside the bed—

KISSY. It *did* rather look like a hunchbacked dwarf, though!

FLAME. That's what *Eloise* thought it was, anyhow!

JERRY. I'm sure the other ladies will be down as soon as they've gotten Eloise back to sleep.

DAN. Very well, then. I'll wrap up a few other matters while we're waiting.

ADLER. Shouldn't *everybody* be here, Lieutenant?

DAN. What I have to say has nothing to do with them or this household.

BUZZY. Then what has it got to do with the *case*?

DAN. That's what I hope to find *out*. (*takes small notebook from pocket, opens it*) Here's some of the information I gathered at headquarters tonight. For starters—*your* name isn't really "*Buzzy*," is it!

BUZZY. Well—no, of course not. It's a nickname. I just happen to prefer it to my *own* name. No crime in that.

FLAME. What *is* your real name, Buzzy?

BUZZY. (*slightly abashed*) "Benjamin Bradford Burdett."

FLAME. (*laughs*) It certainly doesn't *suit* you!

BUZZY. That's why I never *use* it!

KISSY. Quite a monogram it gives you—all *Bs*!

BUZZY. That's how I got the nickname "*Buzzy*"!

JERRY. Dan, this is all fine and dandy, but why bother with nitpicking little details like that?

DAN. You seem to have forgotten Josiah's *will*, Jerry. It's vital we know the *exact* first names of everyone here, remember?

CONNIE. Oh, dear! That's *right*!

KISSY. But Buzzy's real name doesn't change a thing— it still begins with a B! Same thing goes for my *own* name—"Kirsten" and "Kissy" don't affect the will a bit, either!

JERRY. Oh—wait a minute—what a *dope* I've been!

DAN. (*nods*) Yes. You have. I'm coming to that in a minute. But first—(*to FLAME*) Do you *still* want to maintain you're a kindergarten teacher, Miss Fondue?

FLAME. (*stiffens—then relaxes*) I—I guess not. It doesn't much matter any more, does it!

BUZZY. (*as he and KISSY uneasily move slightly away from her*) Who *are* you, then?

DAN. Oh, she's Flame Fondue, all right—except that she's actually a private detective hired two months ago by Josiah Travers!

FLAME. Okay. And what of it?

DAN. Would you mind telling us *why* you were hired by him—?

FLAME. Normally, I *would* mind—client's confidentiality and all that—but if telling what I know might help solve my client's *murder*—! (*shrugs*) I'm *sure* Josie wouldn't mind my providing any information I *can*.

ADLER. And why exactly *were* you hired, then?

FLAME. Josiah suspected *someone* in this household of planning to kill him. He didn't know—or wouldn't *say* — who that person was. He hired me to investigate the lot of them — family *and* servants — to see if *my* findings matched *his* — only he wouldn't *tell* me what he knew — or suspected — until I'd finished my investigation — and before *that* happened — well — you *know* what happened to *him*!

CONNIE. But Flame — what *did* you find out?

FLAME. A certain party was greatly in debt — gambling debts, is my guess — and the only way that person could get any money — especially with a potential jail-sentence looming overhead — was if Josie should *die*. It's no *wonder* he was *worried* about it!

JERRY. You mean the inheritance would cover the gambling debts — ?

FLAME. (*frowns, shakes her head*) That's what I *did* think until tonight — but then, seeing the way the *will* is constructed — I mean, *anyone* can get the money if they can break that *coding* — it doesn't seem to make any *sense*!

DAN. But you came here, regardless, under false pretenses —

FLAME. I wouldn't talk "false pretenses" if I were *you*!

PIPPI. (*comes to her feet*) You mean he's *not* a policeman?!

FLAME. *That* I don't know! I *do* know he's not Dan Denton!

ADLER. *How* do you know?

FLAME. For one thing — I wasn't kidding about that aerobics class — I know Dan Denton quite well. And for another — the *real* Dan Denton was the victim of a hit-and-run driver about six o'clock this evening, just before we all started arriving here!

CONNIE. You mean he's — *dead*?

DAN. Fortunately—no. But he ended up with a lot of bruises and contusions, and will be in the hospital a few days. I was his partner, so I thought it best to attend in his place—I didn't count on Flame knowing Dan, of course.

BUZZY. So *that's* why you looked so surprised when you heard Dan was coming!

FLAME. Naturally! I'd just been talking to him in his hospital room a half-hour before I *arrived* here!

DAN. (*with a wry grin*) Well, thanks for not blowing my cover, Flame.

FLAME. Oh, it wasn't professional courtesy by a long shot. For all I knew, *you* were that hit-run driver. I wanted to see what you were *up* to before I blew the whistle.

PIPPI. Wait a minute—how do we *know* he's what he says? He could *still* be a criminal, *pretending* to be Dan's partner!

JERRY. That's easy, Pippi: When the police got here to investigate the death of Mauvins, they all *knew* him—left him in *charge* of the case—they'd hardly do that with an *imposter*!

BUZZY. (*with mock-sinister tones*) *If* those really *were* the police. . . !

KISSY. Oh, *stop* it, Buzzy! This case is complicated enough already!

BUZZY. Sorry. But say, now, Mister Policeman—what *is* your name?

DAN. David Fescoe, working out of homicide, same as Dan.

PIPPI. (*with a sigh of relief*) Oh, good, that means the *initial's* still the same!

ADLER. Pippi, it wouldn't *matter* even if it *weren't*.

Josiah had *invited* Dan Denton to be present, so it's *his* initial we should *go* by, no matter *what* initial Lieutenant Fescoe had!

PIPPI. Oh. Oh, yes, I see. So everything's still all right, then! (*will sit on lip of armchair-cushion again, as we see THEO and ZITA descending stairs; as they enter parlor:*)

DAVE. However, that brings us to *Jerry* again!

JERRY. (*much abashed*) Don't rub it in! I've been a real idiot!

CONNIE. Jerry, darling, what is Lieutenant Fescoe *talking* about?

THEO. *Who* is Lieutenant *Fescoe*? (*OTHERS look her way.*)

KISSY. Oh, dear, do we have to go all over *that* again?!

BUZZY. Here, *I* can give the gals a quick update—

THEO. Well, I wish you *would*!

BUZZY. While you were gone, it's turned out that Flame is a private detective Josiah hired before his death, and that the real Dan Denton is in the hospital, and this is his partner Dave Fescoe!

ZITA. (*laughs*) This is as bad as missing an installment of a soap-opera! We leave the room for a few minutes, and it's almost impossible to catch up on the story-line!

CONNIE. Nonsense, Zita! I thought Buzzy summed things up quite nicely!

ADLER. Except for the fact that Lieutenant Fescoe was just about to accuse *Jerry* of something when you walked in!

THEO. Then—Eloise was *right*?

DAVE. Right about *what*?

CONNIE. It's *nothing*, Lieutenant, really *nothing*!

DAVE. I'd like to hear about it *anyhow*, if you don't mind!

JERRY. Hell, it's just that Eloise — with fairly good reason, now that I've had time to think it over — got worried that *I*, as a puzzle expert, might be deliberately *mis*interpreting the decoding of Josiah's will, so I could get all the money for *myself*!

DAVE. And — *have* you been?

JERRY. Hardly! I mean, we don't even know if there *is* any money involved!

PIPPI. (*blurts*) But what about the *Swiss francs*?! (*then realizes, cringes, grabs her lower lip between her teeth, shuts her eyes*)

OTHERS. *What* Swiss francs?

PIPPI. (*sighs, stands, waves a hand vaguely toward chart*) Those punctured hot dogs! *Lu* figured it out, hours ago!

JERRY. (*as he and OTHERS all stare at chart*) Swiss francs! Of course! We've been idiots!

CONNIE. It's plain as day, soon as you figure it out, isn't it!

DAVE. Yes, it really is. And *that's* why I think Eloise's suspicions about Jerry are unfounded. (*When OTHERS look his way, curious, he continues:*) With *each* clue we've decoded so far, tonight, it becomes *perfectly* clear that the solution is correct, the moment someone *gets* it! How *could* Jerry be pulling any hanky-panky about it?

ADLER. But — just moments ago — you implied that he *was* up to hanky-panky!

DAVE. No-no, you misunderstood me. What *I* was accusing him of was just plain shortsighted *stupidity*!

CONNIE. (*takes JERRY's arm, fondly*) That's my boy!

BUZZY. And what did my dimwitted buddy *do*, Lieutenant?

DAVE. The same thing *you* did, "Benjamin Bradford Burdett"!

THEO. *Who?*

FLAME. It's Buzzy's *real* name, Mrs. Travers.

KISSY. His initials are three *Bs*—that's why they call him "Buzzy"!

ZITA. Say, that's *cute!*

BUZZY. *I* always thought so!

PIPPI. But what about Mister Delvin? What did *he* do?

DAVE. *Simply went by his nickname* instead of his *actual* name! (*to JERRY*) Shall *I* tell them or will *you*?

JERRY. (*embarrassed, to others*) My *real* first name is "Gerald"!

THEO. But what does it possibly matter what his—? (*It hits her.*) *Oh!*

PIPPI. (*even more agitated as it hits her:*) The *initial's* different! So Lu's got the *wrong number!*

OTHERS. *What?*

DAVE. Pippi—are you telling us that Lucretia has already figured *out* the decoding of the will?

ZITA. (*abruptly*) Say—where *is* Lucretia, anyhow!

ADLER. Oh no! She's probably on her way to Switzerland right *now*, and there's nothing we can do to *stop* her!

JERRY. But we've *got* to stop her!

THEO. Aha! Then you *are* interested in the money!

JERRY. Of *course* I am, wouldn't *you* be?! But what *I* meant was—if she's figured out the *entire* will—she must know the identity of Josiah's *murderer!*

DAVE. Yipe! I never thought of that!

FLAME. Fine detective *you* are!

DAVE. (*moving deskward*) I'll get an APB put out on her! We'll have to alert the airports—!

PIPPI. *Wait!* (*when OTHERS all look her way:*) You don't have to. She hasn't left the house.

ZITA. Then where *is* she?

PIPPI. You've all got to understand—Lu and I made a pact—out in the kitchen, when we were washing up the dinner dishes—we've been friends a long time—and we decided that if either of us could break the code—and know how to get the inheritance—the one who *did* so would *split* with the other one, fifty-fifty.

THEO. But why *should* you?

PIPPI. Because two heads are better than one!

JERRY. Of course! If neither of you had to worry about losing out on the inheritance *entirely*—you could *pool* your ideas, and get to the solution *sooner!*

BUZZY. Okay-okay, we all *get* it! But let's not get side-tracked—where *is* she?!

PIPPI. (*hesitantly*) You understand—I wouldn't betray a friend—except—well, I don't want to be left in the house with a *killer* on the loose, either!

DAVE. You *know* who's the killer?!

PIPPI. No. Lu was just going to tell me when you rang the doorbell. (*moves closetward*) So she hid inside the closet!

FLAME. So *that's* why you were so anxious to hang up Dave's *coat* for him!

PIPPI. (*hand on closet doorknob, now*) I couldn't let *him* go in there, *could* I?!

KISSY. Makes sense to *me!*

PIPPI. (*sighs*) I'm sorry, Lu, but—(*starts opening door*)—I just *had* to tell them—

(*Then door opens fully—that is, its inner surface now
   parallel to the proscenium—and we see LUCRE-
   TIA: She has a short rope around her throat, and is
   hanging on the inside of the closet door from a
   coathook, her eyes wide in shock, jaw slack and
   mouth open; women all SCREAM, and men all
   GASP, and then PIPPI swoons backward and is
   caught by DAVE before she can hit the floor, and
   JERRY and BUZZY hasten to get LUCRETIA off
   the door, remove rope, lay her out on sofa, etc.; all
   this during following speeches:*)

CONNIE. No! *No!*
KISSY. How did it *happen*?!
THEO. Is she *dead*?!
ADLER. (*lurching barward*) I need a *drink!*
ZITA. (*assisting DAVE with unconscious PIPPI*)
Here, let's get her over here into the chair—! (*They will
get her slumped into armchair, move the footstool
nearer chair and put her feet up on it.*)
FLAME. (*peering into closet*) There's nobody *in* here!
BUZZY. (*during business with JERRY and LUCRE-
TIA*) There's *got* to be!
JERRY. (*during same business*) Unless there's some
other way out of there!
DAVE. For Pippi's sake, there'd *better* be!

(*By now, LUCRETIA and PIPPI are in their respective
   locales, and BUZZY is trying to find LUCRETIA's
   pulse.*)

CONNIE. Lieutenant Fescoe—you surely don't think
Pippi killed Lucretia?!
JERRY. That's crazy! Hell, it took me and Buzzy *both*
to lift her off that hook!

KISSY. Pippi could *never* have done it *alone!*

ZITA. (*lays hand on DAVE's arm*) And if she *had* done it, she'd hardly be fool enough to lead us right to the *body*, would she?!

DAVE. (*less certainly*) She *might* have—I mean—since she *knew* we'd find the body sooner or later *anyhow*—?!

FLAME. But if we found it *later*, we'd *never* connect it with *her*, Dave!

THEO. That makes sense, Lieutenant, you must admit—!

DAVE. But—damn it—oh—hell—I guess you're right! Her *faint* was certainly the real thing! Nobody could *fake* turning that pale!

BUZZY. (*releases LUCRETIA's wrist, straightens up*) I'm afraid whoever did this to Lucretia did a good job of it!

CONNIE. She's dead. . . ?

BUZZY. Afraid so.

ZITA. And the identity of the murderer died *with* her!

DAVE. Not necessarily! There was just *one* more bit of information I got at headquarters that practically puts a *spotlight* on the killer!

THEO. *What* information?!

ZITA. *Hurry*, Lieutenant, before somebody gets rid of *you!*

ADLER. (*at bar, has had a drink, fast, on arrival, is now pouring another*) Now, that's the most *sensible* idea I've heard all *night!*

JERRY. Tell us!

CONNIE. Please!

KISSY. Don't *tantalize* us this way!

FLAME. Come on, Dave, *spill* it!

BUZZY. Don't keep it to *yourself*, it's *dangerous!*

DAVE. (*with controlled rage*) I *will*, just as soon as I can get a *word* in *edgewise*!

OTHERS. (*realize they've been impeding him, say in abashed comprehension:*) Oh. . . !

DAVE. (*when silence reigns*) That's more like it! The two major clues are that *stop-sign* and the *gemini* part!

JERRY. Don't give us *hints*, give us the *name*!

DAVE. (*reluctant to just blurt it out, hesitates; then:*) Oh, okay, it's Adler Sheridan!

ADLER. (*drops drink with a crash*) *What*?! You're out of your *mind*!

THEO. Oh, Adler, how *could* you?! Poor old Uncle Josiah—and Mauvins—and Lucretia—!

ADLER. Damn it, Theo, use your *head*! I *couldn't* have killed Lucretia! If she ran into the closet when the doorbell rang, as Pippi asserts, you must all recall that I was *just* coming down the *stairs* with you! And haven't left the room *since*!

CONNIE. Oh, Jerry—he's right! He *was* with us on the stairs!

KISSY. And I'm *sure* he hasn't left the room!

FLAME. Not without one of us *noticing*, that's for sure. . . !

DAVE. But—it *has* to be Adler!

OTHERS. *Why?!*

DAVE. (*goes to chart, exasperated*) Look here! I can tell you *exactly* what the coding refers to!

(*As OTHERS follow DAVE to chart, forming a sort of semicircle behind him-excepting ADLER, who remains back of bar—over on the armchair, PIPPI stirs, opens her eyes, looks around in blank bewilderment as does anyone just coming out of a faint, then tries to get to her feet, and as she does*

*so, she sees LUCRETIA's body on sofa, and reacts
with a LOUD SCREAM, lurching backward till she
supports herself on front edge of phonograph with
the heels of her hands; OTHERS, of course, react
to scream, turn and see her.*)

ZITA. (*running to her*) Pippi, Pippi dear, it's all right,
it's all right!

PIPPI. But she's dead! She's dead! Someone killed
her!

BUZZY. Listen, we *can't* just let her *lie* there like that!
Jerry—?

JERRY. You're right! (*moves around* R. *end of sofa as*
BUZZY *moves around* L. *end*) Let's put her in her
room, on the bed. (*They start to lift her at shoulders
and ankles.*)

DAVE. Hold it! It's against the law to move a body before the police arrive!

FLAME. You *are* the police, Dave!

KISSY. And she's been moved *already*!

THEO. Well, we *couldn't* just leave her *hanging* on the
door!

CONNIE. And what's the point in leaving her *here*,
Lieutenant?

DAN. (*outnumbered and outlogicked*) Oh—okay.
Put her in her room.

THEO. It's just down the hall back of the kitchen—!

JERRY. Thanks! (*He and* BUZZY *will tote LUCRE-
TIA out through kitchen door during next few speeches.*)

ZITA. Sit down, Pippi, please. You've had a terrible
shock!

PIPPI. (*still standing at phonograph, no longer leaning on it*) No . . . no, I'm all right, now . . . it was the
shock—seeing her there on the closet door—and then—

when I came to — I couldn't quite *remember* what had happened for a moment — but when I stood up and *saw* her there — it *all* came back at *once*, and — !

CONNIE. Adler! Don't stand there like a lump! Get her a brandy!

FLAME. (*near bar, goes right to it*) Never mind, *I'll* get it! *You* just stay there in the corner, Adler, where we can all keep an *eye* on you!

ADLER. (*glumly handing brandy bottle and stem-glass to FLAME*) I thought I'd already *demonstrated* that I *couldn't* have done it?! (*JERRY and BUZZY have exited with LUCRETIA by now.*)

KISSY. He *was with* us on the stairs when Dan — I mean Dave — arrived, Flame.

FLAME. (*pouring brandy into glass*) Well, yes, but — I mean — Dave sounded so *certain* — !

DAVE. And I don't see how I can be wrong about it, either — except — Adler's right — if Lucretia ran into the closet just as he was coming down the stairs — damn! Now I'm *all* mixed up!

THEO. Why don't you tell us what you *discovered* — ?

ZITA. What you *thought* you discovered — (*FLAME by now, leaving bottle on bar, is crossing with glass of brandy toward PIPPI, while ZITA drifts up to stand beside THEO, facing toward chart.*)

DAVE. (*no longer so triumphant, sighs, faces chart*) Okay, here we go — ! (*He will point at appropriate parts of chart during:*) Back at headquarters tonight, I followed a hunch I had about that *gemini*-thing that seemed to get a reaction out of Mauvins when it was first mentioned. I rousted a city records clerk out of bed, and had him check back over the past 45-to-50 years for a certain set of *twins* being born!

CONNIE. Twins! Of course!

KISSY. *That's* what gemini means — *The Twins!*

ZITA. But — how *could* you? I mean, there must be twins born at least *once a week* in a city as large as New York — ?!

DAVE. *Not* with one of them named "Adler Sheridan"!

FLAME. (*has given glass to PIPPI, now starts u. toward group*) But Dave, what made you search for *his* name?

DAVE. This stop-sign here! Zero-zero-miles-per-hour! Remember how we couldn't figure out why there were *two* zeroes?

THEO. And why *were* there?

DAVE. Because they're *not* zeroes — they're *Os!* And that sign spells the word "O-O-M-P-H"!

ZITA. Ann *Sheridan!* The *movie* actress!

KISSY. What are you talking about?

THEO. It was before your time, dear. She used to be known as "The *Oomph* Gal"! Just like Clara Bow was "The *It* Girl"!

CONNIE. I don't get it. What does "*oomph*" mean?

THEO. (*delicately*) The — the publicity people at Warner Brothers — well — they indicated it was the sort of *sound* that men would grunt when Miss Sheridan appeared on the *screen!*

KISSY. Oh! . . . Hey, that's neat!

FLAME. (*scanning chart*) So that latter part of the will reads, ". . . I have been — *something* — by *Sheridan*"!

ZITA. (*catching her fervor*) A gemini in this very house"! Of course! No *wonder* Josiah did the will in code! If we could have *seen* Adler's name, Adler would *never* have let us see the will at *all!*

DAVE. But he *had* to, of course, since *he* couldn't figure out where the *money* was at!

ADLER. Really, now, Lieutenant Fescoe, I should explain to you that—

ZITA. Wait a minute! Lieutenant—you said the clue pointed to the *killer*! Where does the code say anything about *killing*?

DAVE. *That* was the *real* toughie to crack! I went over *everything* that could possibly refer to sailors lying in the sun! I mean, a sailor is a seaman—a salt—a tar—a swabbie—and the *other* part—*wow*! Baking—broiling—browning—tanning—reddening—the list goes on and on!

CONNIE. But *what* did you finally *settle* on?

DAVE. The sailor was a "tar" . . . and he was getting himself a "tan"!

ADLER. And *that* makes *me* a *murderer*?! It doesn't even make *sense*!

DAVE. Not until you stop and think where one most often *sees* a tartan!

ZITA. On a scotchman's *kilt*! Of course!

THEO. Of course *what*?! I can't make head nor tails of it!

KISSY. (*who has been scanning chart with the new information, suddenly gasps out, flailing her forefinger at chart*) That's *it*! Dave, that's *got* to be it! (*reads from chart, now:*) "You should also know that I have been *kilt* by Sheridan"!

ADLER. But you're missing one vital *additional* clue in the will!

DAVE. Are you saying it points to someone *else* as the killer?

ADLER. Precisely! . . . The only problem is—that other person could not possibly *be* the murderer!

CONNIE. *What* other person, Adler?

ADLER. (*sighs, then says with quiet bewilderment:*)
My twin brother—Mauvins!

OTHERS except DAVE and PIPPI. *What?!*

(*They move toward ADLER, who is still behind bar;
DAVE remains in chart-area, looking toward AD-
LER; and as they are all focused on the U.R. area,
the panel in the D.L. wall slides silently open behind
PIPPI, and a black-gloved hand holding a dagger
[IMPORTANT: The blade is at the thumb-side of
the hand, not the little-finger side; in other words,
the knife is not held for a down-stab but for a
forward-thrust] comes lancing out of the wall toward PIPPI's back—at the same instant that a nervous ELOISE, in nightgown, robe and slippers, arrives at the foot of the stairs, reacts to the sight she
alone sees, and:*)

ELOISE. Pippi, *look out*!

(*Even as OTHERS look [not toward PIPPI but toward the source of the shout: ELOISE], the hand-
and-dagger whisk back into the wall and the panel
closes—and then an overstressed ELOISE keels
over in a dead faint in the archway area, and OTH-
ERS—even PIPPI, after she gives a bewildered look
round-and-about her area, wondering at the reason
for the scream—rush to pick ELOISE up and try to
get her down to sofa; she is, however, already starting to come to, and she is able to seat herself on the
sofa by the time the group arrives there; during this
interval, from her scream to her arrival on the sofa,
OTHERS should not be silent, but be ad-libbing*)

things on the order of "What happened?" — "Why did
she scream?" — "She said something about Pippi?!",
etc.; *then, once ELOISE is seated at center of sofa:*)

DAVE. Don't crowd her — give her air!

(*As OTHERS move aside a bit — we'll end up with
DAVE, CONNIE, PIPPI and ZITA near* L. *end of
sofa, and THEO ADLER, KISSY and FLAME
near* R. *end of sofa — kitchen door opens and JERRY
and BUZZY rush in.*)

JERRY. What was that scream?
BUZZY. What happened?
ELOISE. Somebody tried to kill Pippi!
PIPPI. *What?!*
THEO. Eloise, dear, you must be *delirious!*
ZITA. No one was anywhere *near* Pippi!
ELOISE. Stop treating me like a mental defective! I
know what I *saw!*
DAVE. And just what exactly *did* you see, Miss Ains-
ley?
ELOISE. A gloved hand — with a dagger — thrusting
toward Pippi's back!
PIPPI. But that's impossible! There was no one any-
where *near* me!
FLAME. *Whose* hand, Eloise?
ELOISE. I'm sorry — from the foot of the stairs, with
the closet jutting out like that — I couldn't see the actual
person — just his hand and arm!
KISSY. But there was nobody there! Pippi was all
alone there, by the phonograph — !
JERRY. (*realizes*) Just like Mauvins — before the lights
went out!

BUZZY. Jer — you mean you think Eloise *did* see somebody?!

CONNIE. With all that's been going on here tonight, *nothing* would surprise *me* any more!

ELOISE. Of *course* I saw somebody! I only wish I could have seen who it was! (*belatedly reacts to CONNIE's statement*) What did you mean — *all* that's been going on here? You don't mean something *else* has happened — *besides* Mauvins' murder?

THEO. (*soothingly*) Now-now, you mustn't overexcite yourself, dear. Why don't you go back up to bed and have a nice —

ELOISE. No way! Not again! I'd barely gotten to sleep when I heard *all* of you screaming, down here! That's what brought me downstairs — I heard screaming, then shouting, then a lot of muffled murmuring — I couldn't *stand* not knowing what happened — (*looks around at group*) Just what *did* happen?

BUZZY. (*after all try to recall for a second*) Aha! That must have been just about the time Pippi opened the closet and we found —

THEO. Buzzy, please!

ELOISE. Theo, will you *stop* fluttering like a mother hen! Found *what*, Buzzy?

BUZZY. Your cook, Lucretia.

ELOISE. . . . Dead?

BUZZY. As a mackerel!

ELOISE. But why would anyone murder our *cook*?!

PIPPI. She said she knew who the *murderer* was!

ELOISE. Who? Who did she say it was?

FLAME. She didn't!

ZITA. And now, poor dear, she never *will* be able to!

DAVE. But as a matter of fact, we think we *know* who killed her!

JERRY. We *do*?

BUZZY. Since *when*?

CONNIE. Oh, that's right, you two weren't in the room when we found out!

JERRY. Found out *what*?

BUZZY. *If* we're not being *nosy*—?!

KISSY. (*babbling on almost in glee*) Dave found out that Mauvins is actually Adler's twin brother! That's what the "gemini" means on the chart! And that sailor is a *tar*, getting a *tan*—!

ZITA. (*with similar relish*) And a *tartan* is on a *kilt*, and "kilt" is a pun on the word "killed"!

THEO. And Ann Sheridan was known as "the *Oomph* Gal"!

BUZZY. What the hell *is* this, a murder investigation or *Trivial Pursuit*?!

FLAME. That's what the speed-limit sign meant, Buzzy—not double-*zero*, but double-*o*! And o-o-m-p-h spells "oomph"!

PIPPI. And Zita remembered that was what they used to call Ann Sheridan—

DAVE. So I had a city records clerk look up twins named Sheridan, and—

JERRY. Hold it, hold it, my head is starting to spin! Are you saying that *Adler* did it?

ADLER. They are all *trying* to—but they are forgetting one other part of Josiah's coded message: It says that the *older* gemini is the one responsible for Josiah's murder! And—if you did your checking in *depth*, Lieutenant—you will see that I am the *younger* twin!

DAVE. (*grabbing out notebook, paging through it rapidly*) That's impossible—everything fits—I can't be mistaken—(*finds place, reads:*) "Sunday, October 31st, in the year nineteen-hundred-and—"

JERRY. Damn it, we *know* Mauvins was born on Halloween, he already *told* us that!

BUZZY. So his twin brother must have been born on the same date! (*OTHERS all look toward BUZZY in exquisite silence; then:*)

FLAME. I always *suspected* you were real bright!

CONNIE. But the *time*, Dave, the time of the *births*—?!

DAVE. (*looks at notes again*) Mauvins Sheridan was born at one-oh-five ay-em that Sunday . . .

ADLER. (*calmly*) That is correct, Lieutenant Fescoe . . . Now read the *next* part!

DAVE. (*from notebook:*) And his twin brother Adler Sheridan was born at—at—(*looks up at group, bewildered*) At one-*fifty* ay-em that Sunday—!

THEO. But—that makes Adler forty-five minutes *younger* than Mauvins!

KISSY. That's crazy! I mean—if Adler is the *younger* gemini—?!

ADLER. Exactly what I was trying to tell you all, earlier: It means that the murderer named in Josiah's will is my twin brother Mauvins!

JERRY. But—Mauvins was killed because he knew the *identity* of the killer—!

DAVE. We can't *know* that—?!

ELOISE. But what *other* reason *could* there be?!

ZITA. This is insane—you're all saying that Mauvins *was* the murderer, according to the will—and that he was stabbed before he could *identify* that murderer! I simply cannot see how he could have been *both*!

CONNIE. Murderer *and* murder victim?! Neither can I!

THEO. Unless . . . ? (*when OTHERS look her way:*) His conscience tormented him until he—he—

DAVE. Killed himself?

ADLER. Theo, *nobody* commits suicide by stabbing themselves in the middle of their own *back*?!

KISSY. Even if they *wanted* to—I don't see how they *could*!

BUZZY. (*to ADLER*) I don't suppose your brother moonlighted as a *contortionist*—?

FLAME. Buzzy, Mauvins had *enough* trouble just *walking* across a *room*, let alone plunging a *dagger* into his own *back*!

BUZZY. But Flame—if we *all* keep insisting that he *didn't* do it—

ELOISE. —then one of *us* did it! (*Very slightly, almost imperceptibly, each person moves fractionally away from everyone else, with a quick and uneasy left-right look of unwilling suspicion.*)

BUZZY. Which means that Josiah Travers' accusation was *incorrect*—!

PIPPI. Which means that the *rest* of the will could be incorrect, *too*! (*All turn slowly, and look toward chart on wall.*)

THEO. Even . . . even the . . . the numbers of that safe deposit box in Lucerne!

ZITA. Well, there's only one way to find *out*! Let's figure *out* those numbers, and see if there *is* such a box!

DAVE. And just which *one* of us do we *trust* enough to fly over to Lucerne and find *out* . . . ?! (*and as all stare at one another in mounting suspicion—*)

THE CURTAIN FALLS

End of Act Two

ACT THREE

*It is about ten minutes later. Closet door is wide open
(JERRY is inside closet, but we cannot see him yet);
BUZZY, FLAME, CONNIE, KISSY and PIPPI
are on barstools, facing U.R. area, drinking and
chatting (but their voices are unheard by us); coffeetable now has coffeepot on it, and—seated on
sofa—THEO, ZITA, ELOISE and ADLER each
have a cup of coffee in hand, and are sipping between bouts of dialogue; DAVE is seated on front
edge of desk, angled in general downstage direc-
tion, talking on telephone; a few seconds after curtain-rise, JERRY emerges from closet, shaking his
head.*

JERRY. Well, folks, if there's a secret exit in that
closet, *I* sure can't find it! (*will shut closet door, and
move barward, during:*)

ZITA. Are you trying to say that *Lucretia* killed herself, *too*?

DAVE. (*on phone*) Yeah, Marty, that's right, *another*
one! . . . No, this time it was strangulation! At least—
hold on a second—! (*turns head barward*) Buzzy—
you're the medical man—it *was* strangulation, wasn't it?

BUZZY. (*half-swivels to face him*) Seems the most
likely cause of death—I mean, that rope around her
neck wasn't *helping* her any!

(*JERRY will arrive at bar, go behind it, and fix himself
a drink, during:*)

DAVE. But you're not *absolutely* sure—?

BUZZY. Hell, Dave, it *could* be some rare South
American *poison*, sure, but why would the killer even
bother? A rope around the windpipe does the trick quite
nicely.

DAVE. (*back on phone*) Marty—? . . . Yeah, it almost *has* to be strangulation. We'll let the medical examiner give us the final verdict . . . How soon can you guys get here? . . . Right . . . See you then. (*hangs up phone, stands*) Fifteen-twenty minutes, he figures.

FLAME. (*swivels to face him, and OTHERS at bar will now turn that way, too*) Oh, good! Leaves us *just* enough time to pretty up before they start *grilling* us again!

JERRY. *Unless* we decide to play *charades*!

PIPPI. How can you all be so *nonchalant* about it?!

BUZZY. We're *not*, really, honey. It's just the mind's way of giving out protection so we don't go bananas— called post-shock syndrome.

CONNIE. It's just easier to get a bit giddy than to face up to the horror, I guess!

KISSY. It beats running in circles and screaming, any day!

ADLER. I think I'd *prefer* hysterics to dumb jokes!

ELOISE. Not me. I've had all the hysterics tonight that I want to have in my lifetime!

THEO. Amen to that!

PIPPI. Has anybody figured out those *numbers* yet?

DAVE. (*moving up to bar area*) Doesn't seem to be much *point* at the moment. You'll all be lucky if they let you leave the *neighborhood*, let alone jaunt across the Atlantic!

FLAME. Hey, buddy, don't forget that restriction includes *you*, too!

DAVE. What are you talking about?!

JERRY. Being on the homicide squad doesn't absolve you as a *suspect*, Dave.

ZITA. Considering the salaries they pay policemen, a box full of Swiss francs could be mighty tempting!

DAVE. Well—that's true enough, I guess—but don't forget I didn't have any opportunity to commit *either* murder!

ELOISE. For that matter, *none* of us did! But two murders *have* been done!

BUZZY. (*leaves drink on bar, moves down toward desk*) Hell, we may as *well* figure out those numbers while we're waiting—

(*FLAME will leave her own drink and move down to stand just U. of desk chair as BUZZY sits and gets pen and pencil and starts figuring; DAVE will continue up to bar, sit on BUZZY's vacated stool, and fix a drink.*)

JERRY. I guess it'd be nice to be able to read the *entire* will, at that! (*will come around end of bar and move down beside FLAME*)

PIPPI. (*to DAVE*) Shouldn't you be refraining from drinking on duty?

DAVE. After watching two *murders* in one night, I don't think even the *police commissioner* would want to stay *totally* sober!

ELOISE. And don't forget the *attempted* murder of Pippi!

JERRY. Say—that's right! And that's *another* puzzling development! (*when OTHERS look his way, curious:*) What was the *motive*? I mean, both Mauvins and Lucretia could have exposed the *killer*—but what did *Pippi* know?

PIPPI. (*when OTHERS look her way, after a moment's silence:*) Nothing! Nothing at all! I mean— nothing that anyone would want to *kill* me about!

ADLER. Of course, we have only Eloise's testimony that there *was* an attempt on Pippi's life!

ELOISE. How dare you? (*slams coffee cup down on coffeetable, stands*) I may not be a spring chicken, Adler, but I'm far from senile! I saw what I saw! It's not *my* fault nobody *else* did!

THEO. Eloise, dear, *no* one is suggesting you were *lying*—just *mistaken.*

BUZZY. (*who has been calculating at desk, sets down pen*) Okay, here's that magic number to make all our dreams come true!

KISSY. (*hops down from stool, moves deskward*) Let's have it then—and I'll race you all to the airport!

FLAME. (*who's been watching what BUZZY has been writing*) Do you want just the numbers, or the whole calculation?

DAVE. May as well give the whole thing; in case there's an error or something, maybe someone'll notice.

BUZZY. Fair enough. Taking us all alphabetically, it goes like this: Adler, Buzzy, Connie, Dan, Eloise, Flame—then we skip G, H, and I—and then we—

ZITA. Wait! Remember that Jerry is actually "Gerald," so—

BUZZY. It doesn't matter. I've got to give old Josiah credit—he must have taken that into account when he *coded* the thing—

THEO. Taken *what* into account, Buzzy?

BUZZY. Which name Jerry would be going by. See, the number itself is *three*—I mean, the missing letters till the next name are G-H-I. But if we *go* by "Gerald," it's *still* three, because we drop the upcoming *J*, and the missing letters become H-I-J, see? There's still three of them, either way.

ADLER. All right, all right, we understand. Just get *on* with it!

BUZZY. Okay. The next group of names are Kissy, Lucretia and Mauvins. Then we skip N and O, which gives us *two* as the next digit—and we move on to Pippi . . . then skip Q-R-S, giving *three* again as the *third* number . . . then comes Theodosia, and we skip through U, V, W, X and Y—giving us the number *five*—and we wrap the alphabet up with Zita!

DAVE. So the safe deposit box number is three-two-three-five and—uh—? *What* was the last part?

ELOISE. Eight-two, as in "*Et tu*, Brute!" minus the brew and the *thé*!

JERRY. (*looks toward chart*) Just for clarification, then, let's see how the entire will reads . . . the way Josiah *intended* it to be read after decoding—

CONNIE. (*turns on barstool, reads from chart:*) "My friends, please bear with me. I belong to a club whose members enjoy dabbling in rebuses, therefore I have decided to leave my vast fortune to anyone—friend, relative or stranger—who can decode this, my last will and testament."

ZITA. (*twisted about on sofa to get good view of chart:*) "You will find a large sum of Swiss francs in a safe deposit box in Lucerne, the number of which is first, initially, the missing letters of this group—"

DAVE. "Three-two-three-five"!

ZITA. "Plus—"

ELOISE. "Eight-two"!

THEO. "Good luck to you all!" And signed "Josiah Travers."

KISSY. "P.S.: You should also know that I have been killed by Sheridan, an older twin in this very house."

ADLER. "Kindly see to the usual legalities in such instances. Jay-Tee." (*to DAVE*) I was *wrong* about that part applying to *me*, as a *lawyer*—actually, it applies to *you*, Lieutenant!

PIPPI. The "usual legalities" being a roundabout way of saying, "Call the cops!"?

FLAME. Nicely put, Pippi!

BUZZY. (*lays pen aside, stands*) So now — seriously — what's our *next* move?

DAVE. What do you mean?

BUZZY. Well, let's say the cops arrive — take Lucretia's body away — and sooner or later the case is declared unsolvable, or something — I mean, somehow we all get off the hook regarding having to *stay* in New York City —

DAVE. Yes — ?

BUZZY. (*shrugs*) Was Kissy *right* awhile ago? I mean, *do* we all race to the airport? Or what?

CONNIE. It *does* seem *odd*, the more I think about it! Much as Josiah enjoyed his constant dabbling into puzzles — I somehow can't see him *really* unleashing a group of frantic travelers in a neck-and-neck gallop to Switzerland . . . !

THEO. It *wouldn't* be like Josiah, no. Of course, Connie, you and I and Kissy have our trust-funds, but — would he *do* that to the *others*?

KISSY. You're right! Would he do such a thing to Aunt Eloise, for instance? I *know* he *liked* her . . . she should get *some* kind of inheritance without having to *scramble* for it — !

JERRY. Same thing goes for the *servants*. Mauvins had given *years* of loyal service — and Pippi and Lucretia rated consideration, too . . .

ELOISE. And what about Adler's *legal* fees?! I mean, isn't a lawyer entitled to a certain percentage of the estate for — well — *handling* matters for the deceased? Doesn't seem fair, somehow, for Josiah to — well — ?

BUZZY. *Stiff* him?

ELOISE. Thank you, Buzzy. Yes, that's exactly what I mean.

FLAME. What you're all saying is that the terms of the will are *not characteristic* of Josie? I have to agree! I didn't know the man *that* long, of course — but it — well — it just isn't *like* him!

PIPPI. But — where does *that* leave us? The chart is certainly intended to mean *something,* isn't it?

ZITA. (*sets coffee cup down, stands slowly*) You don't suppose — it couldn't be that — we've somehow interpreted that coding all *wrong . . . do* you?

DAVE. (*thoughtfully*) Which brings us back to *Eloise's* earlier concern, about — *Jerry!*

JERRY. (*as all eyes zero in on him*) Aw, now — wait a minute — I swear — I mean, of course I don't know for an absolute *certainty* that my various solutions are correct — but don't forget, *I* didn't decode *everything* in this will!

BUZZY. Jerry's right! Why, while he and I were stashing poor Lucretia in her bedroom, you folks had a *field day* romping through the clues! How do *we* know we can trust the *rest* of you?!

CONNIE. But if the will's been misinterpreted — no matter *who* made the errors — what possible *alternative* interpretation could there be?

(*All slowly turn their gazes toward chart and — any remaining sitters now getting to their feet — All slowly move upstage till they are in a semicircle staring at the chart [NOTE: At this juncture, it does not matter if the audience's view of chart is blocked; by now they should be* quite *familiar with all its words and drawings.]; then, after a moment:*)

JERRY. Beats *me* where we could have gone wrong! Anyone *else* have any ideas?

ZITA. Well, look, now — we all know that *some* of the

coding was *simple*—I mean, certain interpretations are blatantly *obvious*, like that "last will and testament" bit. Perhaps if we all eliminated the sections we're absolutely *sure* of, and then concentrated on the parts where a wide variety of interpretations were possible—?

JERRY. That's not bad thinking, Zita, not bad at all!

CONNIE. I agree! Let's take it from the top . . .

BUZZY. Well, far as *I'm* concerned, the first few lines seem almost childishly simple—the bear, the oblongs, the playing-card, arms and legs, buses—any argument there? (*OTHERS ad-lib murmurs indicating they agree.*)

KISSY. And the "therefore"-sign *has* to mean that—

THEO. Actually, everything up through the "last will and testament" seems *unarguably* correct!

PIPPI. But that's where things start getting sticky—I mean, *do* those hot dogs mean Swiss francs? *Is* that vibrating vase capable of meaning nothing but "Lucerne"?

ADLER. And don't forget the "older gemini" bit further along—we *know* that *it* can't be right, since *Mauvins* was older by forty-five minutes!

JERRY. Don't jump around like that—let's stick to one thing at a time, Adler. Now, that trembling bit of crockery, for instance—

ADLER. But I really am concerned about the *twin*-thing, Jerry—!

FLAME. But not awfully concerned about the *twin*, as I recall!

(*Atmosphere in room abruptly shifts, and OTHERS all turn their focus toward ADLER, who backs up a step or two, deskward.*)

ZITA. It *is* odd, now you mention it.

ELOISE. Yes! I mean, if *my* twin brother had been murdered, I'd be a basket-case for weeks!

ADLER. (*defensive-nasty*) Eloise, you're *always* a basket-case! I just don't happen to be the emotional type! I hold my sorrow inside, deep and hidden!

JERRY. Just exactly where *were* you when your brother was murdered, Adler?

ADLER. Why—why I'd left this room much, much earlier—(*to the women concerned*) With Theo and Eloise, *remember*? We were headed for the dining room.

THEO. But you stopped to use the bathroom in the hall, Adler, and we went on without you!

ELOISE. And that's *odd*, come to think of it—when I *arrived* here, Adler had gone there to comb his hair or something—seems strange he'd go back there so soon *again*!

ADLER. This is ridiculous! I killed no one! I wasn't even in the room!

KISSY. That's true, but—actually—(*stops, frowning in puzzlement*)

BUZZY. What is it, Kissy?

CONNIE. Have you thought of something?

KISSY. Mmmm . . . *yes* . . . at least—*sort* of . . .

JERRY. *What*, for pete's sake?! The *last* two people who held information back won't ever be talking *again*!

KISSY. But Jerry, it's *not* information—it's—kind of a nutty *notion*—

ELOISE. Whatever it is, *spill* it, and quickly!

ZITA. Yes, please! The lights go out *far* too easily in *this* house!

KISSY. All right—here it is—for what it's worth . . . I —well—it suddenly struck me as *odd* that, for each murder, it wasn't always the *same* people who couldn't have done it—!

DAVE. Would you run that past me again? I must have missed something.

KISSY. It's only—well—I just got the creepy feeling that—maybe—*more than one* person is in on it!

THEO. Kissy, what are you saying?!

KISSY. Well, when Mauvins was killed, he was far away from *any* of us in this room—Dave was over at the bar, and the rest of us near the desk—and Theo, Eloise and Adler were somewhere *else* in the house—and Pippi and Lucretia were in the kitchen—

ADLER. So what does *that* matter?

KISSY. Well, when *Lucretia* was killed, *again* nobody could have done it! Unless Pippi was lying, Lu was alive when she went into that closet, and mighty dead when she came out—and Pippi wasn't *strong* enough to have hung her up on the door that way—

JERRY. Kissy, we *know* all that. I don't follow you any more than Dave!

FLAME. Hold on—*I'm* starting to get a glimmering . . . neither murder *could* have been done—but we know both murders *were* done—

ELOISE. And Pippi's murder *almost* done!

FLAME. —and the killer *had* to be somebody already in this house—but everybody is perfectly *alibied* for both occasions—which means there has to be a *confederate* in the house, too!

ADLER. Confederate, ha! You're saying the killer was Robert E. Lee?!

ZITA. Adler, there is no call to be flippant!

THEO. Never mind turning the clock back to the Civil War! We need a solution to *today's* problems!

JERRY. (*suddenly wide-eyed*) Ho-lee jumping Jehosaphat! Dave!

DAVE. (*startled at his vehemence*) What?

JERRY. The Sheridan twins — did your records clerk give you their *weights* at birth?

BUZZY. Jerry, have you scuttled your rowboat, or what?

DAVE. (*who has — keeping a wary eye on JERRY while doing so — taken out his notebook again, while he flips pages:*) You *sure* the strain hasn't been too much for you, buddy?

JERRY. Just answer my question!

ADLER. I haven't the vaguest idea what you're driving at, Jerry, but *I* can give you the answer to that question — !

JERRY. Not while you're still a suspect — I'd rather hear it from a cop!

ADLER. How dare you — !

DAVE. Okay, here it is — (*almost reads from notebook, then pauses*) Would you mind telling me what the relative sizes of twin boys has to do with anything — ?

JERRY. As soon as you read me their weights, Lieutenant!

DAVE. (*shrugs, then holds notebook where JERRY can see it*) Mauvins was six pounds four ounces, Adler was six pounds five.

ADLER. (*coldly*) I could have *told* you that! Except for looks, we were practically identical in everything — weight, length, health — !

JERRY. Beautiful! Then that — and Theo's Civil War remark — clinches it!

OTHERS. (*furious at the obliqueness of his statement*) What?!

JERRY. Buzzy — if a woman gives birth to twins — what

is the normal—or at least the average—duration between their births? *If* they are both about the same *size*
and *weight*?

BUZZY. Well, there's no hard-and-fast rule, of course,
but usually about five minutes—fifteen tops. Once she's
sufficiently—

ELOISE. Please, Buzzy! Not in front of the girls!

KISSY. Oh, *honestly*, Eloise!

CONNIE. They teach that stuff in *grammar* school
nowadays!

ELOISE. But I still think that a sense of propriety—!

BUZZY. Let me bowdlerize it a bit, then: Once *one
twin arrives, the way is pretty much cleared* for his *companion* to show up *mighty* fast!

ADLER. (*very nervous, but still with bravado*) That
proves nothing except that our mother had a *very* diffi-
cult time! I think you will agree that an interval of forty-
five minutes is not *impossible*?

BUZZY. He's got us *there*, Jer—!

FLAME. But what in blazes has giving birth got to do
with the Civl War?

JERRY. Not a damn thing!

DAVE. But you said—!?

JERRY. It wasn't what *I* said, it was what *Theo* said!

THEO. Jerry, surely you don't think *I* had anything to
do with—?!

CONNIE. Jerry, you can't *mean* it!

JERRY. Mean *what*? I never accused her of *anything*!

BUZZY. The hell you didn't! We all *heard* you!

JERRY. Oh, hell, not you, *too*?! (*storms away from
group, down into phonograph area*) I was merely trying
to find the flaw in a statement we've all been accepting
without question, and—!

ADLER. I've had enough of these insults! (*strides an-*

grily up behind bar during:) Why would I lie to you about my weight at birth?! And what possible importance could it have?!

JERRY. (*stands with folded arms facing them, back to phonograph*) I should think it would be obvious to *all* of you—!

BUZZY. (*abruptly galvanized*) Look *out*, Jer!

(*And panel has opened, and that arm with gloved hand and dagger moves toward JERRY's back—but he has, at BUZZY's shout, dived face-down on floor—and that arm, hand and dagger* continue *to emerge, parallel to the floor—until the arm is almost* eight feet long; *women are screaming, of course, except for FLAME, who has whipped out a pistol from somewhere and is pointing it at ADLER, forcing him back into* U.R. *corner*)

FLAME. *Freeze*, fella! Or those hot dogs won't be the *only* things with holes.

ELOISE. (*flailing frantic forefinger at the object*) *That's* the thing I saw going for *Pippi*! (*looks a bit more closely, now*) Except it was nowhere *near* as *long* as that!

FLAME. (*still keeping ADLER covered*) Let it go, Sheridan. The game's up!

ADLER. (*releases something down behind bar that we cannot see*) Very well, very well!

(*Immediately, arm-glove-dagger thing reverses course, slides neatly back in through panel, panel closes.*)

JERRY. (*getting up from floor, brushing himself off*) And *that's* how Mauvins' murder was committed!

FLAME. A nifty little gadget, all right! Pull a handle all the way over here at the bar, and the victim gets it, all the way over there by the phonograph!

BUZZY. Sort of a variation on a spear-gun—except, of course, if the dagger *gets* somebody, it remains in the person's back, while the hand-and-arm thing vanishes again.

KISSY. Buzzy! You *knew* about it?

CONNIE. Of course! He *must* have! That's why he faked that argument with Jerry—so Jerry would walk away from the group and tempt Adler to employ that dagger-thing!

JERRY. Right!

THEO. Excuse me, but—

JERRY. Yes?

THEO. What in the *world* does this have to do with the Civil War?

JERRY. (*laughs*) As I've already told you, Mrs. Travers, nothing at all.

BUZZY. It was what you said *about* the Civil War that gave us our clue!

ELOISE. Theo! What *did* you say?

THEO. I—I really can't remember, now . . . it was right after Adler made that snide remark about Robert E. Lee . . . I remember *that* much . . .

JERRY. And you snapped at him about *turning the clock back*! *That's* the *clue* I'd been searching for!

FLAME. I wish you'd explain it to *me*, Jer!

DAVE. Flame, I don't understand—the way you got the drop on Adler, I assumed you were *in* on their plan—?!

FLAME. Not quite all the way, I'm afraid. They'd simply alerted me to get the drop on *whoever* went behind the bar—but why it turned out to be *Adler* I haven't the faintest idea!

PIPPI. Except it means that the will was absolutely *correct* about a *Sheridan* being the killer!

JERRY. Oh, yes, Pippi, very much so! Josiah Travers was a very shrewd man. He'd merely forgotten the significance of the *date* on which the twins were born!

BUZZY. *Fifteen* minutes apart!

ZITA. But—do you mean—Dave *lied* to us?

DAVE. I resent that! I swear, I told you *exactly* what that records clerk told *me*!

JERRY. Relax, Dave. You weren't lying—and neither was that clerk.

CONNIE. Jerry, *will* you explain what you're talking about before I *scream*?!

BUZZY. It's so obvious, we should all be horsewhipped for not seeing it!

DAVE. Seeing *what*?!

JERRY. The twins were born on Halloween—early on a Sunday morning—and that means it was the *last Sunday in October*!

THEO. Jerry, we *know* that much!

JERRY. Yes, but we all forgot one thing: What happens, every year, on the last *Saturday* in October?!

ELOISE. (*the first to get it, after a moment's silence*) We turn the *clocks* back!

PIPPI. Yes, but what has *that* got to do with the last *Sunday*—?!

BUZZY. Because that's the *real* time the clocks get turned back! Most people, of course, *do* it on Saturday night before they go to bed—

JERRY. —but the actual, *official* turnback time is at *two ay-em* Sunday!

DAVE. Hey—are you saying that—?!

BUZZY. Adler Sheridan *was* born at one-fifty, as Dave told us . . . and then, ten minutes later—

CONNIE. (*gets it*) They turned the clocks back to *one* ay-em!

JERRY. And at five minutes *past* one, *Mauvins* Sheridan was born! Which makes *Adler* our "older gemini," just as Josiah told us!

ZITA. I never *did* like having that man around! Now I know *why*!

ELOISE. Jerry, I owe you an apology! I would be *most* pleased to have a *puzzle*-expert as a member of our family! (*suddenly remembers*) Oh! But it *still* doesn't explain the attack on *Pippi*!

DAVE. That's right, Jerry. What motive could Adler have had for trying to use that dagger-gadget on *her*?

THEO. First things first! *I* want to know why Adler murdered *Josiah*!

KISSY. *And* why he felt it necessary to chop him into *seventeen pieces*!

FLAME. Yes, Adler! That *was*—among other things— a bit *excessive*!

ADLER. (*hoists his shoulders in a suave shrug, will come out from behind bar, now—FLAME always keeping him covered—as he explains:*) I will admit—I *did* rather lose my head at the time . . . but what would *you* have done? He had just finished his will—and I knew that I would need my legal fees from his estate to settle all my gambling debts—so as soon as it was completed— since there was no one else but the two of us in the house at the time—I gave him a whack on the head with that cleaver. He died instantly, you'll be relieved to hear. But then—(*His voice tightens and his face darkens.*) —I picked the will up and tried to *read* it!

PIPPI. And you couldn't! No more than the rest of us!

ADLER. Precisely! Furious, I took my rage and frustration out in the only way handy to me at the moment—!

CONNIE. Oh, but Adler—seventeen pieces?!

ADLER. After the first ten whacks, I lost count.

DAVE. Well, that pretty well wraps things up. I'll take over now, Flame. (*draws his pistol, covers ADLER*) But please don't anybody leave the house just yet. When I get back from the police station, I still have a few odds and ends I'd like explained—

JERRY. *I've* got an odd one right *now*, Dave—just *why* are you taking him to the station?

DAVE. Are you serious? He's confessed to murder, hasn't he? And as an officer of the law—

JERRY. Aren't you forgetting that the police are *already* on their *way?*

ZITA. That's right! He phoned them from that very desk just a while ago.

BUZZY. Just a *long* while ago, come to think of it! But if so—where *are* they—?!

DAVE. What are you suggesting?!

FLAME. That your behavior is a bit screwy, for one thing! (*starts for phone*) Let me just *check up* on that phone call—!

DAVE. (*takes backstep so he can cover entire group*) Hold it right there!

JERRY. Then you *did* fake that call!

BUZZY. And pretty cleverly, too! Why, this joker even pretended to be asking *me* details about the *strangulation*!

DAVE. *I* thought that was a nice touch, *myself*!

THEO. I don't understand! What has *Dave* got to do with all this?

ELOISE. Honestly, Theo, sometimes I don't think you've got the brains you were *born* with! Dave is that *confederate* we were postulating!

JERRY. Good for *you*, Eloise!

DAVE. You're acting mighty chipper for a man who's about to die, Jerry. (*to ADLER*) Get Flame's *gun*, damn it! I can't keep them *all* covered at once! (*as ADLER takes gun from reluctant FLAME:*)

ZITA. Wait — if you're going to shoot us — you could at *least* explain why you tried to kill *Pippi*!

DAVE. I could. But why should I bother?

KISSY. That's not *fair*! The villain *always* tells in the *last reel*!

ADLER. Ah, but this *isn't* the last reel, Kissy! This is just the *start*! We dispose of the lot of you — take a pleasant plane-ride to Lucerne — and then —

DAVE. It's not even *that* time-consuming, Adler. The money's *not* in Lucerne!

JERRY. Ah! Then you *caught* that bit, did you?

FLAME. *What* bit?

BUZZY. The misinterpretation of "Lucerne" in the rebus, of course!

ELOISE. Oh! Then you *did* do some hanky-panky, Jerry!

JERRY. Well — yes, I did. But not to *you* — at least, not on *purpose* — I had to keep *Adler* and *Dave* in the dark about it! Sorry I had to flummox the rest of you at the same time.

DAVE. Wait a minute! Are you saying you *knew* I was in on it, even when we were decoding the will?!

JERRY. Yes, but I can't take any credit for that — *Flame* told me!

CONNIE. But how did *Flame* know?

FLAME. I knew even before I *got* here tonight! You

see, Dave, you weren't quite as deft as you thought, getting Dan Denton out of the picture. He *saw* who was driving that hit-and-run car!

DAVE. He couldn't have! I had my scarf across my face, and—! (*stops*) Wow. I really walked into *that* one, *didn't* I!

FLAME. I'll admit I exaggerated slightly. No, he didn't see you at the wheel of the car, Dave—but when I spoke with him at the hospital, he and I were *both* certain that the reason he'd been hit was so someone *else* could come here in his place. I knew who was guilty from the moment you walked into this room.

PIPPI. But I thought he was only pretending to be Dan so that—

BUZZY. Without *telling* Dan what he'd planned to do? Not very likely.

FLAME. And what kind of cop, when his partner's almost killed, doesn't bother to pay him a visit in the hospital?

DAVE. Okay-okay! You're right! For all the good it's going to do you! (*to ADLER*) Let's get it over with, *now*!

KISSY. Wait! Can't you please *explain* a few things, first? I mean, it's not as if the police were *really* on their way!

THEO. You *do* have all the time in the world—

ELOISE. (*glumly*) Even if *we* don't!

DAVE. Yeah, but why *should* I?

ADLER. For *one* thing, Dave—you could explain about the money not being in *Lucerne*! Don't *I* deserve any consideration?

DAVE. Oh . . . damn it . . . all right! (*points across room at stuffed bird*) It's that *sea eagle* there! It belonged to the late cook!

PIPPI. But—Lucretia promised me *I* could have it!

CONNIE. Pippi, what are you talking about?

BUZZY. Hold it! Why would the Travers family let their *cook* keep a *stuffed bird* in the *parlor*?

THEO. It was a gift from Charles, my late husband. *All* these various animals belong to different members of the household. Charles thought they made rather nice *birthday* presents!

BUZZY. (*almost aghast at such stinginess*) And what did the *household* think?

THEO. (*after an exquisite pause*) I'd rather not say.

ADLER. But damn it, Dave—what's that got to do with—?!

JERRY. *I* can tell you that: *Anyone* who's ever solved a lot of puzzles could tell you the name that always crops up defined as a "sea eagle"—it's an *erne*! E-r-n-e, erne!

FLAME. (*gets it*) And it belonged to Lucretia!

PIPPI. (*gets it*) *Lu's erne!*

BUZZY. Right on the button! *That's* what that loose urn referred to!

ZITA. But—if the safe deposit box is in *there*—why bother to give us the *number*?

JERRY. (*shrugs*) *There*, you've *got* me!

ELOISE. Well, why don't we open it up and find *out*?! (*starts toward bird*)

DAVE. Hold it! (*She stops.*) Just stay right where you are. Adler, *you* give it a look!

ADLER. Right! (*hurries over to bird, lifts it from stand, brings it back to coffeetable, sets it down, starts looking for a way into it; all this during:*)

ELOISE. I hate to keep harping on the thing, but—as long as we're all waiting, *anyhow*—*why* did someone try to murder *Pippi*?!

DAVE. When I overheard Lucretia telling her *she*

could keep the bird if something went wrong, I was afraid Pippi might turn all sentimental after her friend was killed—maybe pick the thing up, and discover—

FLAME. Hold it! Backtrack a bit! *When* did you overhear them *talking*?

JERRY. When he was hidden in that closet, shortly before he rang the bell!

DAVE. I congratulate you, Mister Delvin! How did you know?

JERRY. Hell, the secret panel wasn't all *that* hard to find, when I knew there had to *be* one in the closet!

CONNIE. *How* did you know?

JERRY. It was the only explanation for Lucretia's murder: *Pippi* couldn't have hefted that body up onto the door-hook—and the closet was *empty* when we found Lucretia—so there *had* to be another way *in*!

KISSY. But—when you came *out* of the closet, you said you *couldn't* find a secret panel!

BUZZY. Kissy, honey, he didn't want *Dave* to know he'd found it!

ZITA. Why *not*?

JERRY. Because the panel opened onto the *front porch*! And *who* was it that came *in* from that front porch, just moments later?!

THEO. Oh! Why that sneak! That wonderful, lovable sneak!

ELOISE. "Wonderful"?

CONNIE. "Lovable"?

THEO. Oh, stop being so silly, both of you! I didn't mean *Dave*!

OTHERS. Then *who*?

THEO. Why, *Charles*, of course! My late husband! He used to stay out till *all* hours, sometimes, and I'd get very angry and wait for him in the front hall—and so *many* nights I'd suddenly hear him *snoring* — and there he'd be asleep in his favorite armchair, with a book open on his lap!

ELOISE. Do you mean to say — ?

CONNIE. Oh! How very *devious* of Daddy!

KISSY. I can see him now — popping into the closet — ditching his hat and coat — easing out through the closet door —

THEO. And then grabbing a book, sliding into the chair, and snoring so I'd think he'd been there asleep all along!

JERRY. He sounds like a man I'd have liked to have known.

CONNIE. Oh, he was, darling, he was!

ADLER. Ah! Got it! (*back of bird opens, and he pushes it aside, coming to his feet with a large metal box in his hands*) And *here's* why we needed those numbers — ! (*holds up front of box to group*) It's got a *combination-*lock!

DAVE. Well, *open* it and let's get *out* of here!

ADLER. What *were* those numbers, anyhow. . . ?

ZITA. Three-two-three-five-eight-two!

KISSY. *Zita!* As soon as he *opens* that box, they're going to *kill* us!

ZITA. Ah, but Adler is *not* going to open the box!

ADLER. (*turns and looks at her*) Oh? And why not?

ZITA. Because — (*points at him*) *You* are a *frog*! (*And ADLER immediately drops box, and starts frog-hopping all over the downstage area, croaking melancholically.*)

DAVE. Adler, have you gone *crazy*?!

BUZZY. No-no, that was *me* she made into the *idiot*!

FLAME. You should *never* mess with a *gypsy*-type!

DAVE. (*as ZITA turns his way*) *Oh*, no, lady, you don't pull the same trick on *me*! (*takes backstep, near archway, points gun at her*)

THEO. Zita, look out! (*dives onto her friend bodily, and both of them go over back of sofa and roll onto sofa-cushions [if they are* agile *enough, they can continue downward till they're on floor between sofa and coffeetable]*)

JERRY. What *now,* Dave?! Adler's out of commission, and you certainly can't shoot *all* of us!

DAVE. (*eyes blazing with fury*) You're *right,* you stinking super-brain! So, if I *have* to pick and choose my victims with *care*—! (*levels gun directly at JERRY*)

CONNIE. (*leaps into JERRY's arms*) No! Don't!

LUCRETIA. *He* won't! (*She has just stepped into view from* R. *of archway, and stands facing DAVE's back, her hands out of sight behind her own back.*)

OTHERS except DAVE. (*variously:*) Lu!/Lucretia!

DAVE. (*whirls around to face her*) What—?! But— you're *dead!* (*then, with lightning recovery*) But if you're *not,* you're *going* to be! (*raises pistol*—*pulls trigger*—*gun clicks harmlessly*) What the hell—?! (*looks stupidly at his useless weapon*—*and then LUCRETIA brings large iron skillet from behind her back and brings it down upon the top of his head with a very satisfying "Thwoiiing!" [use Sound-Effect here], and DAVE crumples unconscious to the floor*)

PIPPI. Lu! (*Rushes to her, they embrace.*)

LUCRETIA. There-there, honey, it's all right, it's all right!

THEO. Listen—listen, everybody—aren't those *police sirens*—?

(*All pause*—*except ADLER, of course*—*and sure enough, very faintly in the distance, SIRENS can be heard.*)

FLAME. But I thought Dave *faked* that call?!

LUCRETIA. Oh, he did! But there's an extension in my bedroom. I phoned them just before I came out.

KISSY. But Buzzy—when you examined her on the sofa—you said she was *dead*?!

BUZZY. What did you *expect* me to do? Let the killer know he'd goofed, so he could try to kill her *again*?!

ELOISE. Doctor Burdett—you're *much* smarter than you *look*!

BUZZY. Why, shucks, I—(*Then it hits him, and he gives her a suspicious look.*)

JERRY. (*picks up box, takes it toward desk, on:*) Zita, can't you do something about our amphibian friend?

ZITA. Sorry. A frog was the first thing popped into my head—! (*to ADLER*) *You* are a *bran muffin*! (*And —now in area before phonograph—he immediately stops hopping, sits on floor knees-to-chest, and his arms embracing his knees, utterly motionless.*)

BUZZY. Uh—Zita—didn't you *forget* something—?

ZITA. Oh! (*to ADLER again:*) A *breathing* bran muffin! (*He commences breathing.*) Thanks, Buzzy!

PIPPI. Oh, Lu, you took such an awful chance! What if he'd shot you before you clobbered him with the frying pan?!

ZITA. No chance of *that*, my dear! I took the bullets out of his gun *hours* ago! (*toward DAVE's fallen body*) We *gypsy*-types are *very* good pickpockets!

ELOISE. *Hours* ago? You mean, even before he got the *drop* on us?

JERRY. We wanted to be prepared, just in case. I mean, we didn't know *when* he was going to revert to type, exactly—

THEO. But how did *you* know Dave was in cahoots with Adler?

JERRY. Because whoever triggered that dagger-mechanism to kill *Mauvins* had to be in back of the *bar* at the time. And that's where *Dave* was, all by himself — the rest of us were down near the desk.

KISSY. But how did he turn out the *lights* from there?

JERRY. That's where *Adler* came into it; I suspect that — after having gone into the bathroom, leaving the ladies for a moment — he ducked out the bathroom window, came around to the front-porch panel, and reached out of the closet to darken the room — then all he had to do was get *back* to the bathroom while Dave was eliminating Mauvins from the *bar*!

BUZZY. Look, we can iron out the details later! Right now, let's get a look into that *box*!

JERRY. (*will start to dial combination during:*) You're right! After all, the contents of this box is what the entire evening's been *about*!

LUCRETIA. (*moves barward*) And *I* need a *drink*! That noose didn't help my throat one bit!

BUZZY. You're lucky you've got a thick neck!

JERRY. (*finishes dialing*) That's got it! Here goes! (*lifts lid, looks inside box, reacts, shuts lid again*) Well, I'll be darned!

CONNIE. What *is* it, darling?

ELOISE. Aren't the *Swiss francs* there — ?!

JERRY. I'm afraid not!

OTHERS. *What?!*

JERRY. (*points at chart*) It seems we all made one *slight* error about those *holey hot dogs*! That's not what they represent at *all*!

THEO. Then *what*, Jerry?

JERRY. Those aren't hot dogs — those are *pods*! And those aren't holes — they're *seeds*! What Josiah was drawing there is *St. John's Bread*!

ZITA. Isn't that a fancy name for—what is it—the *carob* bean?

JERRY. Right! And—knowing how Josiah luxuriated in *puns*—what does *that* term suggest to you?

PIPPI. *Caribbean?!* Like in the Caribbean *Sea*?

JERRY. Exactly! And, considering the term "sea" in *financial* circles—what would it convey to you. . . ?

KISSY. *One hundred!* Like in a *C*-note! A hundred-dollar bill!

JERRY. Bingo! And in this box, in nice thick packets of one thousand apiece—with one of our names on each packet—we have more *C-notes* than I've ever seen in my life!

ELOISE. We're rich! We're all rich!

JERRY. (*tucks box under his arm*) What do you mean—"*we*"?!

(*And we have an overlapping group-rendition of:*)

CONNIE. Now, honey—!
BUZZY. Aw, Jer—!
PIPPI. You don't *mean* that—!

(*OTHERS can voice similar not-really-so-worried sentiments, but all start moving toward him, their hands outstretched, as he hugs the box now in both arms, protectively, backing away with a big grin, and SIRENS get louder and louder, and—*)

THE CURTAIN FALLS

End of Play

DETAILS OF THE WILL-CHART

To be fair to the audience, the following should be rendered large enough to be read easily from anywhere in the theater:

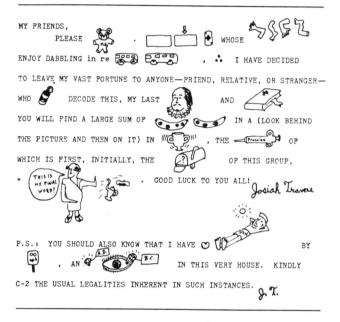

If the foregoing *can* be seen by the entire audience, they cannot argue that they didn't have as much chance as anyone in the play of solving the mystery, when All Becomes Clear in the final act.

MONK FERRIS

(NOTE: The playwright will *not* be offended if you decide to have an artist with *talent* do a re-rendering of that artwork, above, in order to be *absolutely* sure the audience can recognize items.)

SCENE DESIGN
"BONE-CHILLER"

1 DOUBLE SWING DOOR TO KITCHEN
2 LIGHTSWITCH #1
3 PORTRAIT/WALL SAFE
4 DESK/CHAIR/PHONE
6 BAR/STOOLS/LIQUOR SHELF
6 ROLLUP CHART ON WALL
7 LIGHTSWITCH #2
8 ARCHWAY TO FRNT. HALL
9 STAIRS TO BEDROOMS
10 8" PLATFORM
11 FRONT DOOR
12 OUTDOOR BACKDROP
13 PORCH AND RAIL
14 CLOSET
15 LIGHTSWITCH #3
16 LOUNGE CHAIR AND FOOTSTOOL
17 STUFFED BIRD/BOOK-SHELVES
18 SECRET PANEL (1'×1')
19 PHONOGRAPH/RECORDS
20 SOFA AND COFFEE-TABLE

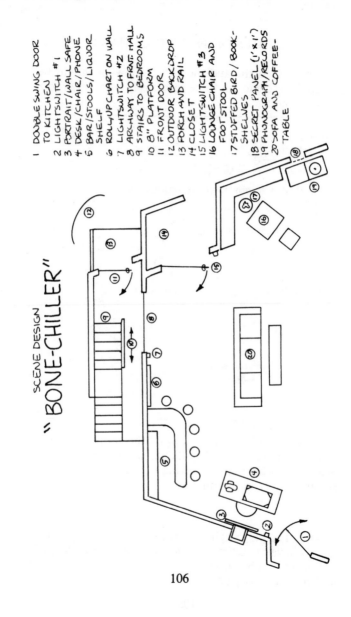

106

Other Publications for Your Interest

GUILTY CONSCIENCE
(LITTLE THEATRE—DRAMA)

By RICHARD LEVINSON and WILLIAM LINK

2 men, 2 women—Interior

Arthur Jamison is a renowned criminal attorney—brilliant, amoral, charmistic, treacherous to friend and foe alike. In this case his friend (about to be ex-friend) is his wife Louise, who is fed up with his endless philandering and manipulations. Arthur, never a procrastinator, begins plotting to kill her. He creates an imaginary prosecutor, a formidable opponent who pokes holes in the seemingly perfect murder schemes that he devises. In the courtroom of his mind, Arthur pits himself against his alter ego in a series of sometimes witty, sometimes hostile exchanges. Again and again he is frustrated, realizing that unless he formulates the ultimate alibi, he will be financially devastated by Louise. To his shock it appears that his wife and someone else are actually planning to kill *him*. But this, of course, just might be just another fantasy. Or is it? ". . . Deathtrap meets Colombo. . . . its premise and devices are clever . . . moments are the stuff of a first-rate case of goosebumps . . . an artful mixture of reality and fantasy. . . ."—Miami Herald. ". . . the playwrights have a dandy time manipulating us into believing one thing, then switch on the lights and merrily exclaim, "Surprise!" . . . Wonderful dialogue and satiric jabs at criminal justice . . ." Miami Sun-Sentinel. ". . . much to recommend . . . abundant humor, intricate puzzles, and pure excapism . . . well worth recommending."—San Diego Leader. ". . . most pleasing and ingenious . . . clever and extremely well-turned . . . accomplishes the considerable task of making us care about its characters . . . skilled craftmanship that sets up certain expectations and fulfills them handsomely."—La Jolla Light.   (#9139)

DEAD WRONG
(LITTLE THEATRE—MYSTERY)

By NICK HALL

3 men, 1 woman—Interior

Worried that his rich wife Peggy will leave him without a penny, Craig Blaisdell devises a cunning plot that will give him control of her money and get rid of her handsome young escort. It's all just a murderously ingenious game to Craig, but the stakes are high and the game turns real. "A model of its kind: witty, suspenseful and neatly plotted right up to its final twist."—Hartford Courant. "Intriguingly written, suspenseful with frequently applied overtones of comedy."—Farmington Valley Herald ". . . keenly written with a provocative and chilling edge . . . the plot twists are enough to out-Christie Agatha."—New England Entertainment Digest.   (#6138)

SAMUEL FRENCH has:
AMERICA'S
FAVORITE COMEDIES

THE MIND WITH THE DIRTY MAN – MOVE OVER, MRS. MARKHAM – MURDER AT THE HOWARD JOHNSON'S – MY DAUGHTER'S RATED "X" – MY HUSBAND'S WILD DESIRES ALMOST DROVE ME MAD – NATALIE NEEDS A NIGHTIE – NEVER GET SMART WITH AN ANGEL – NEVER TOO LATE – THE NORMAN CONQUESTS – NORMAN, IS THAT YOU? – THE ODD COUPLE – THE OWL AND THE PUSSYCAT – PLAY IT AGAIN, SAM – PLAZA SUITE – THE PRISONER OF 2ND AVENUE – P.S., YOUR CAT IS DEAD – THE RAINMAKER – ROMANTIC COMEDY – SAME TIME, NEXT YEAR – SAVE GRAND CENTRAL – SEE HOW THEY RUN – SHRUNKEN HEADS – 6 RMS, RIV VU – THE SQUARE ROOT OF LOVE – SUITEHEARTS – THE SUNSHINE BOYS – TEN NIGHTS IN A BARROOM – THERE'S A GIRL IN MY SOUP – 13 RUE DE L'AMOUR – A THOUSAND CLOWNS – TWO FOR THE SEASAW – VANITIES – WALLY'S CAFE

COUNT DRACULA

TED TILLER

(All Groups) Mystery comedy
7 Men, 2 Women. Interior with Small Inset
1930 Costumes (optional)

Based on Bram Stoker's 19th Century novel, "Dracula." This is a new, witty version of the classic story of a suave vampire whose passion is sinking his teeth into the throats of beautiful young women. Mina, his latest victim, is the ward of Dr. Seward in whose provincial insane asylum the terrifying action transpires. Her finance arrives from London, worried over her strange inertia and trance-like state. Equally concerned is Professor Van Helsing, specialist in rare maladies, who senses the supernatural at work. Added trouble comes from Sybil, Dr. Sewards demented, sherry-tippling sister and from Renfield, a schizophrenic inmate in league with the vampire. But how to trap this ghoul who can transform himself into a bat, materialize from fog, dissolve in mist? There are many surprising but uncomplicated stage effects, mysterious disappearances, secret panels, howling wolves, bats that fly over the audience, an unexpected murder, and magic tricks which include Dracula's vanishing in full view of the spectators.

> Despite much gore, ". . . the play abounds with funny lines. There is nothing in it but entertainment."—*Springfield, Mass. News.*

FRANKENSTEIN

TIM KELLY

(All Groups)

4 Men, 4 Women, Interior

Victor Frankenstein, a brilliant young scientist, returns to his chateau on the shores of Lake Geneva to escape some terrible pursuer. No one can shake free the dark secret that terrifies him. Not his mother, nor his financee Elizabeth, nor his best friend, Henry Clerval. Even the pleading of a gypsy girl accused of murdering Victor's younger brother falls on deaf ears, for Victor has brought into being a "Creature" made from bits and pieces of the dead! The Creature tracks Victor to his sanctuary to demand a bride to share its loneliness—one as wretched as the Creature itself. Against his better judgment, Victor agrees and soon the household is invaded by murder, despair and terror! The play opens on the wedding night of Victor and Elizabeth, the very time the Creature has sworn to kill the scientist for destroying its intended mate, and ends, weeks later, in a horrific climax of dramatic suspense! In between there is enough macabre humor to relieve the mounting tension. Perhaps the truest adaptation of Mary Shelley's classic yet. Simple to stage and a guaranteed audience pleaser.

6 RMS RIV VU
BOB RANDALL
(Little Theatre) Comedy
4 Men, 4 Women, Interior

A vacant apartment with a river view is open for inspection by prospective tenants, and among them are a man and a woman who have never met before. They are the last to leave and, when they get ready to depart, they find that the door is locked and they are shut in. Since they are attractive young people, they find each other interesting and the fact that both are happily married adds to their delight of mutual, yet obviously separate interests.

". . . a Broadway comedy of fun and class, as cheerful as a rising soufflé. A sprightly, happy comedy of charm and humor. Two people playing out a very vital game of love, an attractive fantasy with a precious tincture of truth to it."—*N.Y. Times.*
". . . perfectly charming entertainment, sexy, romantic and funny."—*Women's Wear Daily.*

WHO KILLED SANTA CLAUS?
TERENCE FEELY
(All Groups) Thriller
6 Men, 2 Women, Interior

Barbara Love is a popular television 'auntie'. It is Christmas, and a number of men connected with her are coming to a party. Her secretary, Connie, is also there. Before they arrive she is threatened by a disguised voice on her Ansaphone, and is sent a grotesque 'murdered' doll in a coffin, wearing a dress resembling one of her own. She calls the police, and a handsome detective arrives. Shortly afterwards her guests follow. It becomes apparent that one of those guests is planning to kill her. Or is it the strange young man who turns up unexpectedly, claiming to belong to the publicity department, but unknown to any of the others?

". . . is a thriller with heaps of suspense, surprises, and nattily cleaver turns and twists . . . Mr. Feeley is technically highly skilled in the artificial range of operations, and his dialogue is brilliantly effective."—The Stage. London.

VERONICA'S ROOM

IRA LEVIN
(Little Theatre) Mystery
2 Men, 2 Women, Interior

VERONICA'S ROOM is, in the words of one reviewer, "a chew-up-your-finger-nails thriller-chiller" in which "reality and fantasy are entwined in a totally absorbing spider web of who's-doing-what-to-whom." The heroine of the play is 20-year-old Susan Kerner, a Boston University student who, while dining in a restaurant with Larry Eastwood, a young lawyer, is accosted by a charming elderly Irish couple, Maureen and John Mackey (played on Broadway by Eileen Heckart and Arthur Kennedy). These two are overwhelmed by Susan's almost identical resemblance to Veronica Brabissant, a long-dead daughter of the family for whom they work. Susan and Larry accompany the Mackeys to the Brabissant mansion to see a picture of Veronica, and there, in Veronica's room, which has been preserved as a shrine to her memory, Susan is induced to impersonate Veronica for a few minutes in order to solace the only surviving Brabissant, Veronica's addled sister who lives in the past and believes that Veronica is alive and angry with her. "Just say you're not angry with her," Mrs. Mackey instructs Susan. "It'll be such a blessin' for her!" But once Susan is dressed in Veronica's clothes, and Larry has been escorted downstairs by the Mackeys, Susan finds herself locked in the room and locked in the role of Veronica. Or is she really Veronica, in the year 1935, pretending to be an imaginary Susan?

> The play's twists and turns are, in the words of another critic, "like finding yourself trapped in someone else's nightmare," and "the climax is as jarring as it is surprising." "Neat and elegant thriller."—*Village Voice.*

MY FAT FRIEND

CHARLES LAURENCE
(Little Theatre) Comedy
3 Men, 1 Woman, Interior

Vicky, who runs a bookshop in Hampstead, is a heavyweight. Inevitably she suffers, good-humouredly enough, the slings and arrows of the two characters who share the flat over the shop; a somewhat glum Scottish youth who works in an au pair capacity, and her lodger, a not-so-young homosexual. When a customer—a handsome bronzed man of thirty—seems attracted to her she resolves she will slim by hook or by crook. Aided by her two friends, hard exercise, diet and a graph, she manages to reduce to a stream-lined version of her former self—only to find that it was her rotundity that attracted the handsome book-buyer in the first place. When, on his return, he finds himself confronted by a sylph his disappointment is only too apparent. The newly slim Vicky is left alone once more, to be consoled (up to a point) by her effeminate lodger.

> "*My Fat Friend* is abundant with laughs."—*Times Newsmagazine.* "If you want to laugh go."—*WCBS-TV.*